THE LAWLESS
A TRIPTYCH

MERC FENN WOLFMOOR

ROBOT DINOSAUR PRESS

Robot Dinosaur Press

www.robotdinosaurpress.com

THE LAWLESS: A TRIPTYCH

"Trust In the Law, For the Law Trusts In You" first published in *Ignorance is Strength* ed. John Joseph Adams, Christie Yant, and Hugh Howey (2020)

"Believe In the Law, For the Law Is All" first published in *Burn the Ashes* ed. John Joseph Adams, Christie Yant, and Hugh Howey (2020)

"The Law Is the Plan, and the Plan Is Death" first published in *Or Else the Light* ed. John Joseph Adams, Christie Yant, and Hugh Howey (2020)

Ebook ISBN: 978-1-949936-36-0

Print ISBN: 978-1-949936-46-9

Cover & interior design by Bog Wolf Cover Designs

TRUST IN THE LAW

A Good Citizen follows all the Laws set forth by the benevolent Government. Trust the authority of the State. Questions are against the law.

BELIEVE IN THE LAW

The Government cares about you. The Government wants you to be happy. Do not deviate from the Government's prescribed conditions of happiness.

OBEY ONLY THE LAW

Never question the Law, for that leads to anarchy. Always obey, lest you be found undesirable. Undesirables do not deserve life. And you, Good Citizen, want to live, don't you?

THE LAWLESS: A Triptych collects three tales of near future America, and the people who fight against the totalitarian regime that wants to destroy them — plus a bonus story about resistance in a dystopian nightmare.

CONTENTS

INTRODUCTION

A few years back, John Joseph Adams emailed me to ask if I'd like to write a trio of stories for an anthology triptych—one for the pre-dystopia, one for the "current" dystopia, and one for the post-dystopia. Of course I was like, "Oh HELL YEAH :D" because this sounded awesome and I've loved working with John as an editor.

I sketched out some ideas of how I would construct my triptych of stories, and it went dark very, very fast. This was also during the Trump admin here in the U.S., and working out anger and grief and fear in fiction was one of the few ways I was coping. It took a lot longer than I'd anticipated (my eternal thanks to the editors for being understanding in all this), and the resulting trio of stories that resulted are ones I'm extremely proud of—I poured a lot of rage into these, and possibly it shows, heh.

While the stories are fictional, there have been a terrifying number of moments where they feel more like reality. A depressing, horrifying number of times. I often felt like yelling that fiction was not a blueprint for real-world policies. It's exhausting, this fight. But the thing with fiction is that we get to decide the endings. We don't have to let the bastards win.

And so while these stories are dark as fuck in many regards, ultimately they all end with hope. We will always keep fighting so the darkness cannot win in the end.

Stay safe, my friends. You are not alone.

—Merc Fenn Wolfmoor
April 2022

CONTENT NOTES

acephobia, biphobia, bullying, child death, domestic violence, gore, gun violence, homophobia, intimate partner abuse, mass shootings, mention of surgery, misogyny, murder, police brutality, racism, religious abuse, religiously motived violence, school shootings, state-sanctioned violence, suicidal ideation, suicide (gun-related), transphobia, violence against women

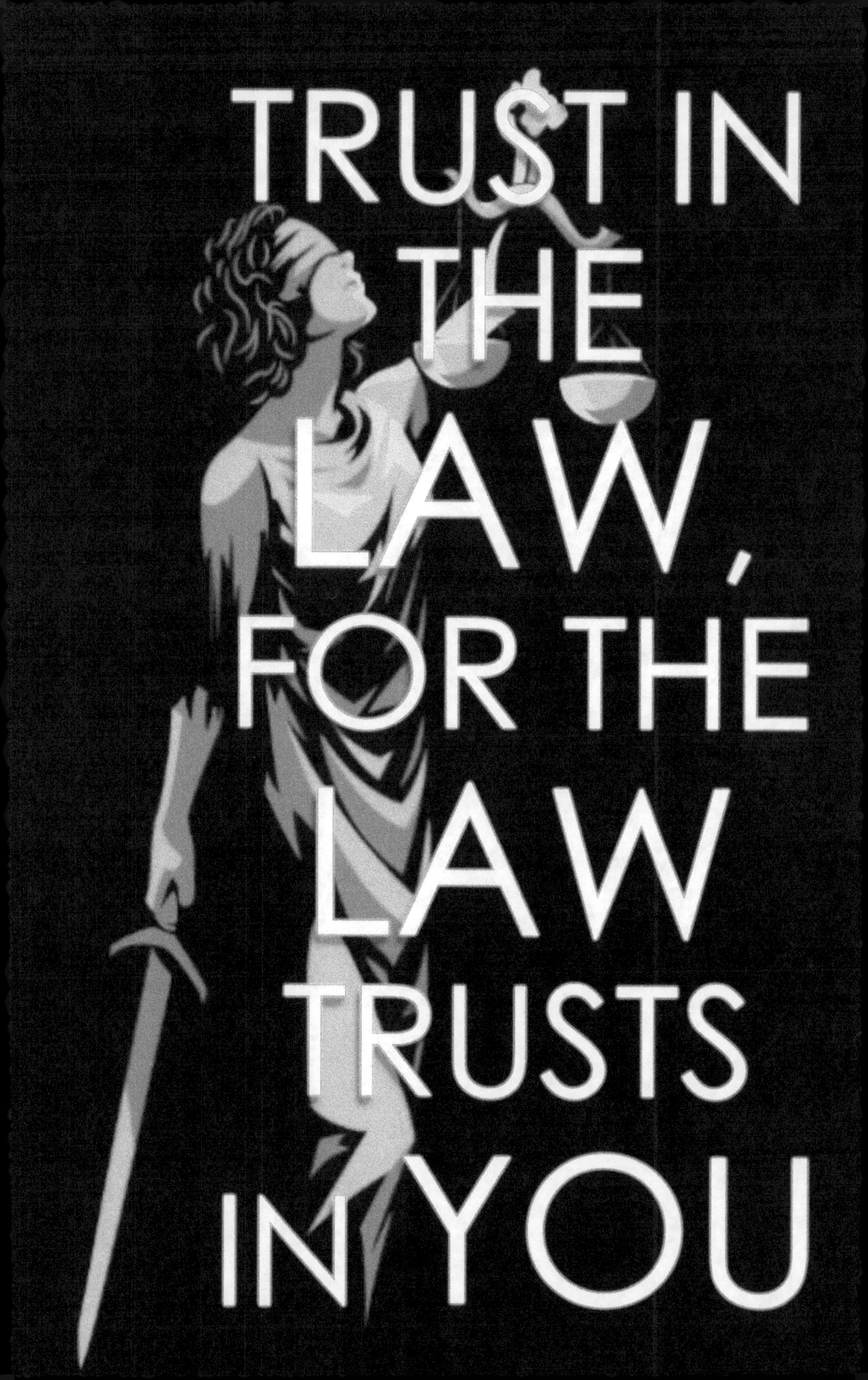

TRUST IN
THE
LAW,
FOR THE
LAW
TRUSTS
IN YOU

TRUST IN THE LAW, FOR THE LAW TRUSTS IN YOU

"Reality exists in the human mind, and nowhere else."

GEORGE ORWELL, 1984

It's the seventy-sixth mass shooting this year, on May 15th, just a block from your school, in a fast food restaurant. Sixteen dead. The panic surges hot and fierce in your throat as tweets flood your timeline. You're so viscerally aware *that could've been me*, but you can't fucking do anything. Like all the other times.

Because if you hadn't been sick today, you would have been in the afternoon crowd grabbing fries and a shake after class.

You text your friends and check Instagram, desperate to know who was there, who's dead, who's spared this time. Your phone vibrates non-stop as people check in, as people beg to know if you're okay. *I'm at home, I'm fine,* you reply constantly. Soon your phone's auto-fill populates the text field as soon as you tap the letter I.

A migraine pulses behind your eyes, so you mute your phone and crawl under the covers, praying you won't vomit on the sheets because you've got three days before Aunt Dora can afford to do laundry this week.

You've attended too many fucking funerals this year.

"The U.S. Department of Education, in conjunction with private sector tech companies, launches a new and innovative program to combat the epidemic of gun violence," reports Kelly Sun. The blonde morning anchor for FXNews. "VISIONS, which stands for Virtual Inclusive Socialized and Integrated Online National Schooling, is a virtual reality augment. It will be conducted in safe, secure facilities and tap into cutting edge technology that will allow students to learn and interact in a safe environment. Early beta tests report that the experience within VISIONS is so life-like, that you can't tell the difference once inside the simulators.

Local high school King's Academy has been approved as the first public school to incorporate VISIONS into the required curriculum beginning in September…"

A year comes and goes. VISIONS is instituted in your school. In truth, you like the VR—it's remarkably fluid and within the virtual classrooms, there are easy hacks to text your friends without visible phones, so the teachers never notice. And in the VR, you can modify your avatar, wear a body that *fits*, that is sculpted to who you are.

VISIONS doesn't stop the news, though. When you finish the period and disconnect from the headset, reality comes back. More shootings.

A daycare. A night club. A laundromat. Another synagogue. An anonymous grief support group. The local mall. Two mosques. A Lutheran church. A hardware store. Three different playgrounds.

Nothing changes.

The worst thing about helplessness is how much is takes from you. By June you're so tired you can't even move out of bed. Summer vacation is a sick joke.

On July 4th, the president's daughter—who was attending a charity auction in a swanky hotel—dies in the one hundredth mass shooting this year. One of the banquets staff was murdered and impersonated so the shooter could bypass security in the ballroom. No one ever notices the service workers.

Finally, those in authority do something. No one bans or regulates gun, nah, no one is going *that* far in this glorious U.S. of A. Instead, VISIONS is launched nationwide. It's suggested for cooperate and business sectors. There is historic funding to push through VISIONS as part of the Department of Defense's budget for homeland security. Within two years, it's estimated, the virtual reality networking will part of everyday life; an overlay on reality.

There are promises: you'll be able to see guns like X-ray vision, and thus take proactive steps to defend yourself or be the hero. All social and financial interactions can take place through the overlays, etc. It will be a safe future, proclaim the ads and the spokespeople and conglomerates who flock to throw money at propagation of the new tech.

The September you're a senior at King's Academy High School, things change.

It should feel momentous: the last leg of your journey before you're an adult. Next comes college, a career, marriage, a family, financial security, happiness, all that bullshit the older generations want to shove down your throat as the ideal. Too bad it's all lies, and you can't swallow any of it.

Your best friend, Danielle, chair of the student council, proposes that King's Academy hold a fundraiser talent show to benefit the students who were most impacted by gun violence this summer. Thoughts and prayers don't cover medical bills or funerary costs.

"You can choreograph something, Arren," Danielle says, volunteering you in her usual enthusiastic way.

Before the summer threw you into a depressive loop, you used to love choreographing dance and stage fights for the theater club. You took ballet lessons until you were nine, until the pressure to perform femininity became too unbearable and you dropped out, taking up computer programming instead.

Danielle believes in you, or at least she has no one else who'll do it, so you agree.

This is a great excuse to ask Peter Ritter to participate: mister too-handsome-for-his-own-good swim team star, and surprisingly skilled vocalist in his indie metal band. You have no idea if he's straight or not, considering he flirts with anything that moves but hasn't officially hooked up with anyone, and even if he isn't, it's not like he'll notice *you*. Geeky, shy, hella awkward trans guy destined for a college degree in computer science and a career in IT.

It takes you a full three days to work up the nerve, so on Friday, with the cover of "Do it for the greater good! Help us raise money!" you approach him in the hall as he's sauntering to the locker room, waving and joking with everyone he passes.

"Hey Pete?"

Goddammit, why does your voice still have that squeak. You've been on T for ten months now, because Aunt Dora is a flaming liberal, your legal guardian, and she's supportive of her nephew's bodily autonomy. She's believed you since you first came out to her at eleven. Your dad would be rolling in his grave if he ever knew. Mom hasn't been in the picture since you were a toddler, so fuck her.

"Arren!" Pete grins, extending a hand for you to fist-bump. "What up, man?"

Your face heats, even if you straighten a bit more and smile back. It's so goddamn validating when people casually call you man. Pete has zero self-consciousness. He's so charismatic, so considerate, so...unavailable.

"Um, I'm helping Danielle Yu organize a show..."

"Right!" Pete's expression mellows to appropriate solemnity. "For the fundraiser."

You nod, heart pounding. Pete Ritter is talking to you and you need to keep it professional, dammit. You memorized your notes on how to proceed and still your brain is doing summersaults into the land of *how is he so fucking hot.* "Do you know Tess Ogakanna? She's going to do an ASL performance of Disturbed's 'The Sound of Silence,' and we're looking for a vocalist to accompany her. You'd appear as a silhouette behind her."

Pete's eyes light up. "Shit, for real? Tess is awesome!"

People shuffle and hustle past you, and you're hyper-aware that a lot of the girls are eyeing you and Pete, and some of the jocks are making rude gestures. You fix your eyes on Pete's gorgeous face: the perfect cheekbones, the strong jaw, the wide mouth. His eyes are this rich, drown-yourself-forever brown.

"Arren?"

Fuck! "Sorry," you blurt, realizing you've been ogling him right to his fucking face. "Do you think, um, you might want to help out with Tess's performance? I'm choreo-graphing the look of the set, and, uh…"

"Dude, I'd love to! That song is like my total jam." He grins again, easy and already forgetting how you were staring like an idiot ten seconds ago. "Hit me up on messenger this evening, okay? We'll hash the deets then." He gives you this hilariously cute little salute, then sweeps off, catching Becky Chow's arm and giving her an exaggerated kiss on the cheek. She laughs and punches him in the arm, though not very hard.

You quickly make yourself disappear before you melt from embarrassment.

"Let's do it in VISIONS," Danielle says. She's lying on her stomach across your bed, rapid-texting on her phone. You swivel your chair and stare at her. Your dual monitors cast a harsh, LED glow across the room. All the other lights are off, since it's three a.m. and Aunt Dora thinks you're asleep.

"Why?"

It's two weeks before the fundraiser, and she wants to do it in VR now?

"Look," Danielle says, "I know Ben the gaffer is great and all, but we just don't have the equipment or skill to pull this off. Principal Uptight isn't going to approve actually spending money." She rolls her eyes. "Hell, it was him blathering on about costs and budget and image that gave me the idea."

Principal Upton is a miser, especially when every department needs funding, all the teachers are exhausted and underpaid, and only the football team seems to get new gear each season. The tech corporation that developed VISIONS, C-Sun Inc., donated all the tech and the student-use hardware. C-Sun has been systematically making grants available—ridiculously fast, honestly—to any student over the age of fifteen who will agree to try the new chip implants that link into the VISIONS system. Paired with glasses, the chip shares real-time biometric data and updates, and lets you see the augmented overlays. You're hoping to get top surgery, you're on HRT, and so right now, you don't care to have additional implants messing you up. The glasses are enough. Besides, you can't forget the one bad press case that got around: when a student enrolled in beta piloting, only to suffer a stroke when she failed a live-shooter drill in VR. It's not happened again, but the danger is always there. Maybe you're just paranoid.

VISIONS is big enough that it could easily draw enough people, especially with King's Academy being the poster school for the program. Performing in VR might get you some corporate generosity. A nice tax-deductible donation for the families of victims.

"If we marketed it, we could also get some national attention," you say, pushing aside your misgivings. "More viewers mean more potential donations..."

"See? I'm brilliant." Danielle shrugs. "Plus, I want to invite my dad, but he's still out of the country."

Oh, right. He's not in Beijing by choice.

"Okay," you say. "Let's do it in VISIONS."

You're just behind the edge of the curtains, stage right, watching as your piece—the finale of the show—unfolds. You feel like you're in the auditorium, even though physically you're hooked up in one of the VISIONS hubs at school. The whole show is being streamed online, in hopes of securing a huge audience. Everyone with a VISIONS chip or physical interface—glasses or headsets—can experience the event as if they are there. Otherwise, it'll look like a regular 3D video when viewed on a screen. Somehow, Principal Upton got the Governor herself to attend the virtual event, and so her PR team is giving your school a huge boost. It helps that this is an election cycle.

Tess, dressed in a brilliant white three-piece suit and a pearlescent half mask—a costume from last year's *Phantom of the Opera* production, Raoul's outfit and Erik's mask—

walks slowly to center stage. A spotlight follows her; she glows. Her ebony hair is a tight coil atop her head, and she wears black stilettos that echo-click on the floor.

In VISIONS, every visual is enhanced into super high definition. Colors pop. Sounds are so crisp you can almost taste them. The velour of the curtain is soft against your fingers, and the only thing missing is the stink of sweat, old gum, vape smoke and stale perfume. You honestly don't miss the olfactory mess of being backstage.

The first notes in F sharp minor fill the air, Tess stops center stage, head bowed, arms at her sides. The whole backdrop is a tight white screen. Peter appears behind it as a silhouette, just to Tess's left. He begins singing, his voice a growly baritone that aches with repressed sorrow and rage.

The vibrato ripples along your skin and quickens your pulse.

Tess signs in ASL as Pete sings; the screen behind her slowly resolves into a photorealistic scenic set: a rainy street, glistening stones, a single streetlight poised right above Tess. Always, Pete's outline is barely visible, even as his voice carries. As the song continues, you remind yourself to breathe.

The background changes seamlessly between landscapes, color washes, and at the lyrics "ten thousand people, maybe more," Peter's silhouette is duplicated until the layered shadows black out the screen. The scene fades back into a wasteland, and Tess, alone, keeps signing.

Tess's expressive language and body movement rivets the

performance. As Pete's voice climbs in the final verse, Tess's spotlight turns scarlet and she's bathed in bloody light, her costume illuminated like the Red Death.

Pete's voice fades on the words "the sound of," and while the music continues, there are no vocals. Tess spells out S-I-L-E-N-C-E with one hand and when she's done, she drops her arms to her sides and the entire stage goes black.

A moment of breathless quiet, so appropriate, and then as the lights raise and Pete steps up to take a bow beside Tess. Thunderous applause shakes the auditorium. The echoes thrum under your shoes. It's so loud and yet in VISIONS, it doesn't physically hurt your ears. The viewers online must be in the millions now. You clap furiously, your palms tingling, your face aching from the perpetual grin.

The audience is on its feet, cheering, whooping. Tess and Pete beckon you to join them. You flush but shuffle out It's not nearly as gut-churning as if you were physically on stage, but the nerves are still there. Pete's grin infects you, and you try to keep it cool, and not stare at the sweat-damp locks of hair that curl over his forehead. Tess and Pete applaud you, and you take a bow. The lights aren't washing out your vision.

You can see the front row.

You see the man who isn't clapping, who isn't smiling, who's wearing a heavy black trench coat. His eyes are sunken and rage-filled. His arm reaches under his coat. The fabric flares out, and you're staring at the AK-47.

Time slows, frozen, as the moment of absolute terror

unfolds. He's going to murder you, your friends, the audience. Excessive trauma inside VISIONS hubs will result in neurological damage, because of the interface connections between your mind and body.

You're right in front of the gunman. Above him. He's looking at Tess, not you, and gut instinct tells you she's going to die first. You and Pete will follow in seconds. That's all it takes, right? Seconds.

No.

No more.

No more fucking funerals.

You hurl yourself off the stage, shouting "Gun!" and you smash into the man. The impact takes your breath. You're not large, you're not a hero, but you're solid and scared and furious and you have surprise on your side. Your shoulder drives into his face. Something cracks. You fall forward, he pitches back, stopped by the auditorium's old red-upholstered chairs. Physics hold up in in VR. You wrap your arms around his head, yelling for all you're worth, and drive your knee into his gut, trying to smash his groin. The stock of the AK-47 bashes your kneecap. The pain barely registers.

People flee, screaming. Lights strobe, alarms shrill. Then suddenly Pete is beside you—you smell his cologne, hear him swearing—and then Tess, and all three of you are pummeling this motherfucker and he's grunting and he can't get his hand on the trigger because Tess wields her stiletto like a club, pounding his arm and hand. The man's breath is hot and wet on your armpit. He's trying to bite you. Too bad you're wearing that old leather jacket Aunt Dora bought you for your birthday.

Then the principal is there, and the gym teacher, and a lagging security guard, and someone shouts at you to stop as hands pry you lose. In the back of your mind, you know this is not entirely real—he's in VISIONS, he's somehow manipulated the VR to give himself a gun, he was going to murder everyone—

You stagger back, your binder riding up under your shirt —a detail you wish VR could avoid—your hands and leg and ribs tingling. Pete and Tess catch you. You jump as Pete's hand rests on your shoulder, and he's saying, "Are you okay? Are you okay?"

You nod, wobbling. You finally get a solid look at the scene: the three adults have the gunman pinned on his face on the floor. A wad of chewed bubblegum glares pink and sticky by his temple. The security guard has cuffs out, snipping them onto the man's wrists. Sirens wail outside.

It takes a moment before you realize that Principal Upton also has a handgun, drawn and leveled at the would-be-shooter's head. You had no idea he carried. Your stomach does a sick lurch-flip.

"Let's go, man," Pete is saying, and Tess has whipped off her mask and is signing so fast you can't keep up. Danielle rushes from backstage, her eyes wild. She grabs your arm, and you repeat how you're fine, how no one is hurt. You technically have to exit the auditorium to trigger the

VISIONS hub to disengage. It's supposed to be a security measure.

You stagger away between Danielle and Pete. You glance back once: the security guard and the gym teacher are standing on either side of Principal Upton, who still has his gun. Somehow, the security guy got the perp's automatic rifle and is disassembling it. Why hasn't anyone in the VISIONS admin team not force-quit the simulation and let everyone go?

Just as you turn away, you hear the distinct snik-pop of a silenced shot. You flinch.

"He was going to escape," Principal Upton says, angry, and your head aches like a motherfucker and you don't dare look back and see the blood. It's not real, you tell yourself.

It's all a simulation.

You're called into Principal Upton's office the next day before classes begin. Since the shooter didn't massacre half your classmates, there's no need to allow a day off to decompress.

"Look who it is, the hero of the hour," Principle Upton says, gesturing you to take a seat from him across the desk.

You flush, keeping your gaze down, and sit on the edge of the chair. You bounce your leg, pent up nervous energy making the fidgeting worse. You barely slept once you got home. Danielle stayed over to keep you company and assure Aunt Dora no one was hurt.

"What you did was very brave," the principal continues.

You shrug, embarrassed. You've never liked the scrutiny of attention. You like to be in the background, making things work, helping people without being noticed. "It wasn't real."

But Principal Upton points at the flat screen TV on the wall, his eyebrows arched. You glance over your shoulder, and he unmutes the feed.

The recorded show begins with a clip of Tess and Pete's performance, but it's slightly altered: instead of a full 3D experience exported from the VISIONS servers, this is flattened and condensed to look like cell phone video. It cuts to another angle that shows you leaping off the stage to tackle the gunman. Another cut to the adults having secured the threat and you and your friends standing by. Then the news anchor returns, her face radiant as she breathlessly declares that the heroic students saved their classmates from certain death, and that the principal, Mr. Gerald Upton, performed a great service when he shot the gunman, who was about to escape. There is no footage of that miraculous break-away before a bullet to the head.

"It was very real," says Principal Upton.

Your mouth dries up. What the hell? Everyone knew the show was produced in the VR framework—you swear you saw the marketing. Would there have been a gunman in the auditorium if you'd performed the show in physical space? The convenience of this narrative itches the back of your mind. That perfect take-down, that immediate and useful response from the teachers and security. The dead would-be-shooter.

This is how we prevent mass violence, the TV trumpets, by arming teachers and training students via VISIONS to proactively protect themselves. That's what the launch of VR schooling was for. Safety. Defense.

But it was already in VISIONS. Your tongue feels dry and sticky. What is going on?

"Now, Arren," Principle Upton continues, and you jerk your gaze back to his face. He mutes the news. "I need you to tell me what happened."

Your thoughts spin, like you've just got off one of the spiny rides at Six Flags. "Sorry, what? You saw…"

"I need you to tell me, Arren." His eyes are icy, hard, and you don't know if he carries a concealed handgun in real life. Probably he does. You can't see his lower body from over the desk.

Your pulse thunders. Fuck. You aren't stupid. It hits you suddenly: the threat is right there, couched in false concern. Stick to the story. Don't try to be a hero outside of the VR.

"You know we've catered to your…gender fantasy," he goes on, his voice dripping saccharine condescension. "Now that you have national attention, you wouldn't want everyone to know you're actually a girl, would you?"

It's hard to breathe. He might as well have just kicked you in the guts.

"The world isn't very understanding of deviants," the

principal says, pinning you with his stare, "especially with recent laws. I wouldn't want you to get in trouble."

You swallow. *Don't puke, don't puke, don't puke.* It's all you can focus on. Not vomiting all over his desk, even though it might be satisfying in retrospect.

Aunt Dora went to bat for you to get your school records to publicly show you as male, even though you haven't gotten your ID changed. Thanks to the fuckwads in government, it's getting harder and harder to access legal and medical aid for transitioning. You just hoped to get through high school, do a crowd-funded campaign to pay for top surgery and continued HRT once you're eighteen, and figure out the rest of the shit later.

You're a guy. You've known since you were nine. You've lived your reality since middle school, with Aunt Dora's help, and pretty much everyone now knows you're a guy. Hell, the only people you've told are Danielle and Tess and your friend Marley, who moved last year back to Wisconsin.

"Are you hearing me, Arren?" Principle Upton says, jerking your attention fully back into this godforsaken office with the awards and certificates on the walls, the glossy bookshelves, the huge bay window behind the desk. Posh, as Aunt Dora would say.

"Yes, sir." You clench your itchy hands on your knees. It takes all your concentration to focus on making words that don't sound like babble. "A gunman attacked the school during our talent show. I, um. I surprised him. You and Mr.

VanDassan subdued him. He was killed, but no one else was hurt."

It wasn't real.

Principle Upton smiles like a shark. "Exactly. That wasn't so hard, was it?"

You shake your head. You want to punch him in that fake-smiley face and break all his teeth. "No, sir."

"Good, good. Listen, you'll be getting your own PR team, and a counselor who'll be guiding you in the upcoming press conferences. I've arranged for a private tutor for you, to keep up your grades and studies while on tour, and through VISIONS mobile, you'll be able to stay in touch with your classmates." This is all news to you, but you don't have any shock left. Even the anger is cooling into a depressive pit of acid in your stomach. "You're now the face of this school, Arren. Make us proud."

The media circuit is brutal. Most of your publicity is via the VR interface, allowing you to be on talk shows and give interviews without traveling too much. Your coordinator/liaison/mentor is a decent woman named Claudia Vasquez, who is frazzled ninety percent of the time. But she does her best to be kind and answer your questions in an honest manner. You know she's just doing her job. She has fifty billion tons of pressure on her, too, making sure you look good and stick to the script.

Pete gets his own cycle of fame, especially on the sports channels. Turns out he once went hunting with his father and practiced at a shooting range when younger. Never mind that he's anti-gun ownership now. He's been offered full-ride scholarships to his top schools, but he's declared—in a move you never saw coming—that he's going to join the Army right after graduation. He says it with a smile, but his eyes are hollow.

Tess gets ignored. She's on one local talk-show with her text-to-speech assistive device, but apparently no one in the national media wants to learn ASL or hire an interpreter. Plus, Tess being a Black girl probably doesn't help.

Claudia is supposed to monitor your social media, your private messages, email, phone calls and video chat, and anything else that could potentially allow for leaks. You have three months of being seventeen left to go—the principal and the pro-gun lobbyists are going to milk the ever-living shit out of your story before you're legally an adult and can tell them to fuck off. You tell yourself you're going with this circus performance because of the financial aid Aunt Dora receives. She's paying off credit card bills without juggling late fees and interest charges for the first time in ten years. But Claudia's so busy that she often forgets to check in with you, and your interest in programming—okay, yes, and hacking, it's not like you're ashamed of that—lets you hide your trail.

You don't realize how tired you are until you make a fatal mistake.

It's another interview on a cable news show, rehashing the same story, your brain numb from the bright lights and your face itching with make-up for camera. This is one of the rare in-person interviews the station paid for, flying you on a private airplane to the studio. You are relieved to avoid the TSA.

The host is the blonde white woman, Kelly Sun, who has a brilliant smile and negative compassion. She barely glances at you while you sit uncomfortably on the neon-orange couch on the sound stage. The producer cues you up. You picture the digital lower third banners flaring across millions of TV screens: Arren Darden, Heroic Survivor of King's Academy. You wish Pete was here; it's weird neither of you have been interviewed together. You fix a smile and then the show is live, or as close to live as the networks will ever allow.

"I have with me here the heroic young man from King's Academy today," Kelly Sun says, "Arren Darden, a senior whose actions saved the lives of hundreds of his classmates just a month ago. Welcome, Arren."

"Thanks, Kelly."

You have a beige earpiece fitted to let Claudia coach you off-screen. She gets really into the groove when she guides you, the only time she's ever focused.

"You've been vocally supportive of the VISIONS initiative, which you credit to making you prepared for real-life heroics," Kelly Sun says. You nod, because this is a familiar lie. "With the new law passed today..."

In your ear, Claudia fills you in: "VISIONS-training is being mandated to all U.S. citizens in the public sector, not just school-age kids."

You nod along. You've been hearing about these proposals for weeks. It comes on the back of social media pushes for VR, for connecting people closer and more intimately, so that the country will be safer as a result. There have been a lot of new laws passed lately. None of them involve banning assault weapons.

"How do you feel about the clause that will require all teachers to be armed by next year?"

You blink, horrified. "What?"

Claudia swears and then regains her cool. "Okay, so it was buried in the legalese but yes, all teachers K-12 will be required to carry in order to keep their licenses..."

Kelly Sun gives you a patronizing smile that's like a nonverbal head pat. "Surely you are grateful that Mr. Upton prevented any further violence from the shooter."

"He didn't kill anyone," you say, and Kelly Sun tilts her head a fraction.

"Oh? I think it's pretty clear from the police report that the shooter was killed in self-defense."

"Stay calm," Claudia says. "You can amend with 'didn't kill anyone who didn't deserve it,' that will go over well with the polling audience—"

"He didn't even exist," you snap. "There was no shooter."

Now Kelly Sun leans forward, a cougar smelling fresh

meat. "Can you elaborate? According to all the evidence, your actions helped prevent a massacre."

"Backtrack *now*," Claudia says, panic inching into her voice. Social media must be blowing up. Hashtag: Arren is a liar. "You're stressed because of too much homework and—"

You glare into Kelly Sun's face. All the repressed fear and guilt and overwhelming horror explodes out of you, like a xenomorph chest-buster. "There. Was. No. Shooter." You turn towards the cameras. "The entire performance happened inside VISIONS. This is propaganda. You know what won't stop a real-life shooting? Teachers being armed! Upton murdered someone in cold blood, even if the shooter wasn't real."

"What the fuck, Arren?" Claudia is in full-on panic mode. "Someone cut the feed, go to a commercial, whatever, get him *off the air*."

It's too late. Cable news is like a great white shark, scenting blood, going into a frenzy for chum. And you're treading water with an open wound.

You clench your fists, fighting to keep your voice steady. No going back. Fuck fuck *fuck*. "Gerald Upton threatened me if I didn't spin the story his way. These new laws aren't going to fix what's wrong here."

"Arren! Shut! Up!" Claudia hisses.

You pull out your earpiece and drop it on the floor.

"And what do you think is wrong, exactly?" Kelly Sun asks. She's soaking in the drama, absolutely radiating satisfaction at how her ratings will spike with this segment.

You suck in a breath. You're already screwed. You can't let your terror show. Like that frozen, endless moment in the auditorium, you act. Speak. "More guns aren't the solution. More guns will just mean more bodies in the ground, more funerals, more sensational stories. You don't want to *fix* the problem, Miss Sun, because you *are* the problem. The media spins, the gun lobbyists in government, the warmongers—the problem is America, and VISIONS is only going to make it worse. Because no one will be able to tell what's real and what's not soon."

Claudia must have gotten her way because the producer is signaling Kelly Sun to segue into a commercial or some shit, and you bolt off the stage and straight into your liaison. Claudia catches you by the arms, her face ashen, her hair wild.

"What the hell, Arren? You're going to get me fired—fuck." She shakes her head, holding onto you now more for support than to reprimand you. "Are you okay?"

You're partially in shock. That detached numbness: an outsider's clarity as you assess the situation. The emotional impact will detonate as soon as you let yourself feel and not think.

"I'm fine," you tell Claudia. Your voice is a nasally, flat echo in your head. "Can we go home?"

The fallout is crushing, an avalanche of hate that snowballs in milliseconds. Your social media accounts are overwhelmed with vitriol, with accusations, with rape and death threats. Almost immediately you realize you've been doxxed: Aunt Dora's address is plastered on forums, and equally terrifying, some troll has posted your birth certificate and ID.

You're being called a cunt and a whore and a liar. You shut off your phone. Claudia demands an armed escort—irony's a bitch—for the shuttle ride to the plane, and you want to laugh, but it'd just turn into a scream.

No longer are you the media's pet interview subject. Now you're a colluder and a threat. Because you wanted to be honest and you're scared, and now the whole world wants you as dead as the King's Academy shooter who never was.

Danielle is waiting with Aunt Dora at the police station, since apparently your aunt's apartment is awash with reporters. You huddle in on yourself as your bodyguards shove their way through the crowd and let you inside. You're not even sure why you're here, where it's never been safe, even when you're white. You settle in a little glass and brick interrogation room, but at least you're not handcuffed.

"Oh my god, Arren," Danielle says, hugging you tight. Aunt Dora is arguing with Claudia and the officers outside. Danielle offers you a bottle of water and you gulp it down, even though you'll have to pee super bad and you have no idea if anyone will let you near the men's restrooms. You wish Pete was here; he's the type who would deflect the tension and scrutiny from anyone who looked uncomfortable. You've seen him do it enough, casually intervening between the bullies and the bullied.

"Why'd you do that?" Danielle asks finally, once you've sucked in enough oxygen to power a hot air balloon to the moon and back. "What were you thinking?"

"I just..." But you have no answer.

Danielle shakes her head and hugs you again. You lean against her. She smells like that sweet apple blossom conditioner and you can't help it, you start crying as everything bubbles over in a wave. She rocks you back and forth and makes shushing noises until you've bawled yourself out and your eyes are puffy and sore.

You sit with her on the floor with your backs to the two-way glass wall.

"Sorry," Danielle says, squeezing your hand. "I'm a jerk."

"No," you manage with a sniff. "You're here, aren't you?"

"Sticking by you like a bro," Danielle says. "The reason everyone is mad is because you're right, and they all know it." She gives the room the finger. "You've been used. You and Pete and Tess, hell, all of us. It's fucked, right? Lawmakers shoving their bullshit through the system because we're getting paraded around like sock puppets."

You shrug. What else can you do? Your future is decidedly screwed. If Upton even lets you graduate, no college will take you now: even the offers of acceptance can be rescinded. You doubt you can even go outside safely now. What if the school sues you for defamation? It's not like a public defense attorney is going to do much.

"Arren, listen." Danielle leans her mouth close to your ear and whispers. "A couple of our darknet friends messaged me. You cracked something a hell of a lot bigger open."

You stare at her sidelong, trying to keep your expression from betraying you. Maybe the puffy eyes and snot-damp nose and rumpled hair will fool whoever is watching you through the two-way glass.

"VISIONS is just a first step," Danielle says. "There's something massive in the works: a collusion of big data and the government and VR companies."

"So?"

"So be careful," Danielle says, as the door opens and the officers and Claudia and Aunt Dora all file in. Danielle squeezes your hand once more but says nothing else.

You're in protective custody for the next month and a half. It's agony. At least Claudia was easier to dodge: now you have half a dozen pros monitoring your online presence, any communication, hell, even when you piss. Your testosterone was confiscated. You focus on homework, but it's hopeless. Your concentration is shot. Danielle and Tess visit, but all your friends look haggard. Pete is joining the army; you wonder if he has a choice in that. Tess is moving to live with her grandparents in Canada, since she has dual citizenship. Danielle has made no long-term plans.

Time progresses, inevitable, interminable. Before you know it, it's a week until graduation. You're be allowed to join the processional, cap and gown and everything.

You just want to sleep until the world ends. Maybe it'll go out in a blaze of gunfire or nukes, a Hollywood grand finale that will make all the right-wing nutjobs happy even as they die of radiation poisoning.

Aunt Dora, despite everything, is her usual firebrand self. She keeps you fed, makes you take showers, chases off reporters, and reassures you that you'll both get through this.

"I protested the ever-loving shit out things when I was your age," she says, like a mantra. "Got my ass thrown in jail more than once!"

"How do you go on?" you mumble, staring at yourself in the mirror while Aunt Dora fusses about, gathering laundry.

"So the bastards don't win," Aunt Dora says. She meets your eyes. "They only win when we stop fighting."

You curl up under your blankets. It's hard to stand, let alone fight.

Two days before graduation. There have been thirteen mass school shootings since the show at King's Academy. In three cases, it was initiated by a teacher. The laws remain unchanged.

The news, however, lauds the progress of VISIONS and how it is preparing people of all ages to navigate a fraught world with confidence and ease. Maybe no one can see the house burning down because everyone is already in hell and the only thing that exists is fire.

Danielle shows up at your door with a huge, fake grin and a homemade cake. "Happy birthday, bro!"

You let her in, confused. Aunt Dora is at work, and you're down to one officer for protection now. He sits looking bored in a squad car on the curb.

"It's not my..." you begin, and she barks a laugh.

"Dummy, it's *my* birthday."

That makes equally no sense. Her birthday was in October. "Sorry, Danni, I—"

She winks at you. "Shut up and eat celebratory cake with me." She adds in a whisper, "We need to talk."

Using paper plates and plastic forks, you and Danielle sit on the floor of your room, devouring the cheap yellow box cake with chocolate frosting.

Danielle pulls out a notebook and mutters, "Put on some music," so you cue up your Disturbed playlist on the ancient laptop and blast it from tinny speakers.

Danielle writes longhand, then hands you the notebook, pressing a finger to her lips. Your neck prickles. You know you're under surveillance, online and off, but this seems ridiculously paranoid.

Danielle's note reads:

I intercepted an assassination plot. Aimed at you. There's going to be a shooting at our grad ceremony. You're the target. You'll die "protecting fellow students" in a final act of redemption. Upton will kill the shooter, but only too late. I think he's in on this. And it'll be live, not in VISIONS.

The cake sticks in a lump in your throat.

You take the pen and scribble, *What do I do?*

Danielle crosses out "I" and emphatically scratches "WE."

Then she chews on the pen cap.

You shut your eyes a moment. You have an idea, one that has wormed into your thoughts for days now. A bold, terrible idea—now crystalized with the stark threat on your life. It puts Danielle at risk, but if it works? You will direct the narrative.

You look at your best friend and take the pen. *Up for another performance? Because I have an idea.*

She lights the candles from the cake and holds the paper to the flame. You grab a wire mesh garbage can so she doesn't burn her fingers or the carpet.

It's overcast, but the graduation ceremony is held inside the gymnasium, all echoing walls and slick floors. Hundreds of rows of metal folding chairs in near lines. A stage planted in front of the basketball hoops. Overhead, a massive digital screen looms: it's used for scores, replays, and announcements. News, too, lately.

Music blares, all patriotic horns and militaristic drums and soaring brassy notes. The graduating class processes down the aisle between chairs, stands for a photo, then waits as Principle Upton strides to the podium to make a speech.

You don't give him the chance. You stare out at the crowd, your black gown and cap immaculate, your expression defiant.

"You know what's real." Your voice is firm, calm. You've pitched as low as you can at your register while still being coherent, and you're proud of how it sounds. "I'm real. So are you. In the near future, people will try and tell you that what you know is a lie. There will be authorities who want to gaslight you and trap you in false ideas. There will be many who want to hurt you, even kill you, for knowing your own truth. There's a quote about it getting darkest before dawn. We're in the midnight phase. But the light will come again. Until the sun is back, we have flashlights. Cell phones. Floodlamps. We can make the darkness reveal the truth. Disturb the silence, guys. Fight. There are more than ten thousand of us. We can be heard." You turn your back to the crowd: you've painted RESIST in white letters outlined in red on the gown; the paint dripped a bit, so it looks like blood.

The gymnasium is silent before the roar of voices.

You're not actually there in person: this is the video Danielle filmed on her phone and shunted over to the AV department at school. It was embedded carefully in the scrolling announcements and congratulatory statements on screen. Your voice reaches out through the whole echoing room. You imagine Principle Upton spluttering, furious, yelling at someone to cut the power or turn off that monitor.

Danielle will tell you later, sending messages through encrypted text, that there was no shooting. There was a rippling tension in the air, a sort of expectation that was never fulfilled. After the screen went dark, the ceremony continued, but no one would be the same. Even Upton's speech about being good citizens and obeying the law couldn't dim what you said.

You're far away. Sitting in a rickety old 4x4 Jeep beside Aunt Dora, who's snoring on your shoulder. The landscape reels past you in an overflowing mural. This is Danielle and Tess's and Pete's work. They know folks who know folks. A woman named Farah, a surgeon who worked at an out of state clinic, picked you up at midnight. A cis guy who could do a reasonable impersonation of you made an appearance of getting into Danielle's car in gown and cap; he'll ditch his costume and makeup and never walk into the gym. The police escort followed the false trail. By then, you and Aunt Dora were hundreds of miles away. You've shaved your head and wear color contacts, courtesy of an old make-up kit in your closet.

Danielle records and screens the entire graduation ceremony into her VISIONS account, and posts photos on all her social media. She's a rising star, an internet sensation. Your video hits all the streaming sites and torrents within hours of the ceremony.

You don't know what's coming next. Dr. Farah can get you access to hormones again, so you'll be back on T within a week. She's also connecting you with underground, off-grid anarchists who are willing to shelter you and Aunt Dora while you both get new identities. Aunt Dora is pumped as fuck, her words, for a new adventure. You're too tired to process everything now, and that's okay. You'll have time, because you have a future again.

It's darker, sure, and you know the world is going to get worse. You'll be like a lighthouse in the storm.

Your voice is out there. So is Danielle's, and Tess's, and Pete's, and everyone else who has been harmed. You will not be erased. You will not be made un-real. You'll survive. You'll learn to work behind the scenes, like you've always preferred.

You'll be choreographing resistance.

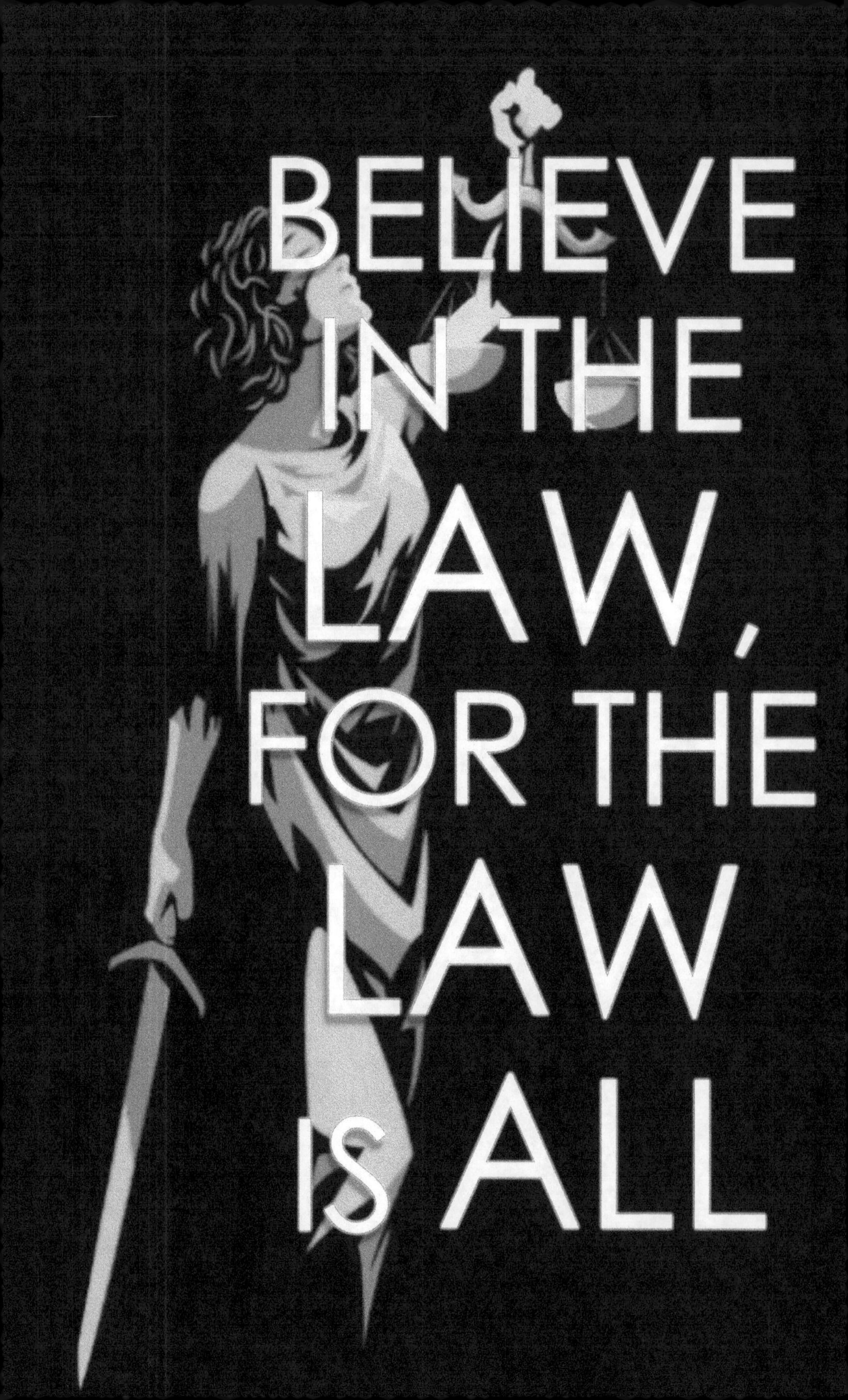

BELIEVE
IN THE
LAW,
FOR THE
LAW
IS ALL

BELIEVE IN THE LAW, FOR THE LAW IS ALL

"For we know that the law is spiritual: but I am carnal, sold under sin."

ROMANS 7:14, KJV

I'm having an identity crisis, so I keep smiling. Nothing else matters but this perfect facade. My husband talks to work associates, so I keep my arm twined about his, my gaze submissive, and I laugh when he makes a joke. I don't even have to process his words; it's a blur of familiar auditory feedback.

The woman attached to the other man's arm is like my mirror-self: brunette, curvy, dressed in a modest one-piece dress with a high neckline and long sleeves. She wears red pumps that showcase her calves. Her eyes are blue, bright like the sky after sunrise.

I want to kiss her.

This is absurd. I'm a normal woman: totally straight. In love with my husband. I can't have these traitorous *thoughts*, and I can't shake the feeling she's eyeing me the same way.

She sends me a private message.

That freaks me out almost as much as the heat in my stomach and the itchy tension in my ribs. How did she get my access code? That's private—we aren't mutuals and only men of authority can ping a strange woman. The four of us stand in the plaza of Behold Eden, Inc., a pristine fountain burbling placidly nearby with a couple visitors tossing pennies into the water. People flow around and past us: a kaleidoscope of public feeds and open statuses, the prestigious citizens lit up like neon signs. There's nowhere to run or hide from a hack. I swallow, my pulse thumping in my ears.

My husband hasn't noticed. Thank the Lord. I turn my head away to cough politely and blink my subfeed on.

Hi, Marley. I'm Dinah.

That's it? She committed a level four social violation to introduce herself? Unless there's a trojan embedded and my firewalls are compromised and—

I'm not going to harm you. Sorry for the deception. You look so uncomfortable.

I keep my smile locked and focus on regaining my

composure. **What do you want?** I shoot back, and risk meeting her gaze.

She smiles a touch wider. **Your husband is about to be sacked. He doesn't know it yet. You deserve a forewarning.**

Sacked? By whom?

Joel is a top-performing admin in Behold Eden, Inc., an upstanding Christian man, a dedicated citizen. His social scores are in the highest percentile. He's due for a service promotion in our congregation next month. The only flaw is me: I haven't gotten pregnant yet, and we've been married for three years. My social score is barely scraping the underside of 89%.

He's going to take a fall for the company, Dinah replies. **And when he does, you'll be dead too.**

Oh my God, oh my God—

Listen, I send, and tag my message #indignation, **whatever game you're playing, I'll report you.**

But then I realize Joel's looking at me, his smooth jaw jutting in anger.

I offer a placating smile. "Sorry, honey, I'm getting a migraine again. What did you say?"

His muscles relax under my hand. He's sympathetic to my headaches and it's an easy cover, even if today it's a lie.

"How does dinner on Monday with Mr. Ritter and his wife sound?"

Mr. Ritter is former military, a decorated war hero according to his overlay; now he's a digital security consult for Behold Eden, Inc. He's handsome, certainly: slicked hair, a tailored suit, attenuative posture. His citizenship score is 100%. Good credit, excellent connections, stellar performance on all civic duty tests. Dinah Ritter is a blazing 97% citscore. I'm getting flutters in my belly again.

Mr. Ritter looks at me, a faint smile softening his expression, and there's a surprising lack of sexual appraisal in his gaze. He's focused on my eyes. His are kind.

"Lovely," I say, glancing up at Joel.

"Monday at six, then," Joel says, and shakes Mr. Ritter's hand.

I don't look at Dinah. Mrs. Ritter. I don't dare. A dull throb pulses behind my eye sockets. Now I'll end up with a migraine for real. The price of lies, Pastor Snow would say. I should have paid attention to my husband.

Joel turns and leads me back to our cab, and the clearest image in my mind is the shape of Dinah's lips.

"These headaches you get," Joel says once we get home. "They're unbefitting." He takes off his suit jacket and loosens his tie; sweat patches darken the fabric under his arms. His cologne is still sharp. "You embarrassed me today."

"I'm sorry." I wipe my palms on my skirt. "I'd never lie to you. That's a sin." I step around him. Our front hall is narrow, lined with digital frames of Bible verses and our wedding portraits.

He reaches out and snatches my wrist. I tense.

"I'm going to ask Dr. Hobbs if your meds might be interfering with our conception."

Why this sudden change in topic? He hasn't talked about our barrenness in a month.

As a man, he's not obligated to smile at all times. My cheeks hurt.

I laugh, and it sounds brittle even to me. His grip is tight but not painful. Not yet. "I want a baby as much as you do." I can't tag my vocal modulation, but I try for #sincerity. "For the Lord and our Great Country. I'd never do anything to harm you, Joel."

"Well there's nothing wrong with *me*," Joel snaps, dropping my arm. He's always kept his Citizen's United Social Networking overlay—CUSN for short—taciturn: his mood never varies from Diligent, and his citizenship score radiates as 100%. The overlay crowning him like a halo is such a different picture than the man in the flesh.

I back into the wall, breathing quicker. "I know, dear."

"Go get lunch ready."

I hurry into our little condo's kitchen. Autopilot only works for so long before the intrusive thoughts kick in: the memory of Dinah's mouth, that spark in her eyes, the smell of her perfume—lilac and lavender.

Get it together, Marley. You're a good, faithful, normal...wife. You're thirty-three years old. Past your prime, maybe, but still fertile. You owe your husband children. You owe society the next generation. This is your purpose. To obey the Church, to serve and to uplift your husband, to honor God.

I'm not a twenty-something anymore. All that talk of rebellion and resistance was a phase in my teens, like my goth make-up and dressing like a guy. I grew up. It's because of VISIONS and the Conservative Prosperity Mandates, and Pastor Snow, that I escaped such a life of sin.

I have a good husband who has a good job, I have a solid if not spectacular social profile, I have plenty of women friends (most of whom have children now), and I have a day-to-day routine that keeps me productive. I have time to study the Bible and the certified CPM texts, watch the daily updates from the President and the Holy Minister. I'm *fine*.

I pull a pre-made lasagna from the freezer and toss it in the oven. My hands shake. I splash some water on my face. The cold is a momentary relief from the tightening pressure under my skin. The pain in my temples burns hotter now. I don't have more than two doses of my anti-migraine pills. And if Joel is paranoid I'm being untruthful with him, he can cancel my refills. Or worse, order a physical exam.

Again, my thoughts flash to Dinah: I don't even remember the context for us meeting the Ritters today. Joel and I had just come from a charity service to benefit Christian soldiers who were killed in the war, dying as martyrs to preach the Good Word and defend America.

Your husband will be sacked. You'll be dead.

None of this makes any sense. Why am I in danger? I've done nothing wrong. My juvie record was expunged.

No, don't go there. That was fifteen years ago. Sometimes it doesn't seem so long—like my youth was a blink in time when I was different, when I was—

STOP IT, Marley.

"Hey, honey," Joel calls from the living room. His voice has a strange edge to it. Alerts ping my feed: something big has happened, and it's not good. I dismiss the push icons. The flashy light worsens my headache.

I straighten, gripping the sink edge. Everything is fine. I'm fretting over nothing. The oven timer tells me our lunch will be ready in five minutes. "Yes, dear?"

"Come watch the news."

All channels blast the breaking story: a massive virus has been detected in the Citizen's United Social Networking system, the official government-mandated augmented reality overlay.

"The cyberattack has opened vulnerabilities in users' CUSN profiles," reports Kelly Sun, a stunning blonde anchor on FXNews. "According to our sources, users may, and I quote, 'be able to alter the gender marker in a profile.' Like name, date of birth, and citizenship, gender fields are locked and immutable. This enormous hack has us questioning: what next?"

CUSN (pronounced "cousin") is an offshoot of VISIONS, the schooling program, and it now connects everyone in the United States. Profiles are public. Your social status and ranking affects your credit, your grades, your financial well-being, your job prospects, and everything else. Only citizens can connect to CUSN, which keeps out the illegitimate influences of unauthorized global non-users. It's freedom of speech manifest: everyone has a voice, and all voices are equal. Naturally some voices are more equal than others, and those with a high CUSN score—like my husband—can hold jobs in government, churches, corporations, and entertainment.

I sink down onto the couch beside Joel, my stomach a knot.

"We must remind all viewers that tampering with the core of your profile is a felony offense," Kelly Sun says. "Do not attempt to manipulate your profile during this cyberattack. CUSN programmers are working on a patch and strengthening the security functions for everyone's safety."

I glance sidelong at Joel. His expression remains stoic.

"That's right, Kelly," says Daniel Brown, the lead anchor. "We've also got a report that the criminal responsible for this horrendous attack on our country is an off-grid hacker named Arren Darden."

A black pixelated box with a white question-mark pops into the corner of the screen.

"No other information is known about this criminal beside the name…" the anchor drones on, but my ears ring.

I know him: Arren was a friend of mine from high school. We lost touch before graduation, but Arren was a sweet, smart guy—he told me he was trans before he disappeared.

Lord, I haven't thought of that word in years. It's illegal. Arren Darden was—is?—a deviant. Why would he do this? Why would he attach his *name* to this kind of crime?

Joel's knuckles whiten, his fists balled on his knees. "Anyone who messes with the order of God should die," he says.

I barely hide my flinch.

"Don't you think, Marley?" Joel stares at me, his jaw clenched.

I nod, my throat tight. I can't disagree with my husband.

"We should hunt them all down and shoot 'em," Joel says.

"I have to go check the lasagna," I say, and stumble back to the kitchen. Only white men are allowed to own guns, so Joel has a permit. He's always been an avid hunter. My hands shake so hard I fumble to turn off the oven timer.

I'm terrified of guns. We're safe in Church because Pastor Snow and all the deacons carry. But when I'm grocery shopping? Or doing errands? I never know.

We're supposed to be better now, as a country, as a society. Every adult white male being required to own a firearm has made the Great United States secure. There are stories all the time on CUSN about the hero with a gun killing the maniac and saving people. Somehow, there are always casualties and funerals.

If hackers can access our CUSN profiles, what's next?

Viruses to crash automated cars? Criminals changing someone's profile to make them look deviant?

It's legal to shoot deviants if you are threatened by one. I remember Arren's cute smile and his nasally laugh and how much he loved programming and the time he told me he had a crush on another boy.

I can see Joel aiming a gun at Arren's face and pulling the trigger.

Smoke seeps out the oven door. I forgot to shut off the heat when I nixed the timer. The lasagna is only slightly burned.

I used to love computers. Gaming, VR, coding. It was a way to get out of the physical world and still *be*. Online you could become someone, you could be authentic and also perform a facade. Branding, it was called.

I know now I was wrong. It was all sin. Even if it felt *good*, maybe especially because it brought me joy.

When CUSN became mandatory and anyone with a record or history of questionable user experience got flagged, I ditched everything and tried to be good. I returned to the Church I'd rebelled against as an ignorant, wayward teen. I strove to be an upstanding citizen. I would prove I could be ideal and gain a high social score. I'd be successful.

Then riots broke out all over. I was at work as a cashier, just getting off shift, when the violence exploded. I was trampled. Concussed and a broken arm. Bad rap. If not for Pastor Snow, I'd have been jailed. But he vouched for me, took me in, matched me with Joel Leighton. We dated for six years.

I willingly forgot so much of my past and myself so I could survive. I believed I'd be happy one day; Pastor Snow and God promised that. I waited and hoped and prayed. I married a man. I sometimes even enjoyed sex with him—I wasn't a virgin, but he didn't have to know. I'd already repented for my sinful ways, and surely God understood. The Son of God talked with harlots.

Sometimes when I dream, I see my younger self screaming behind bars, surrounded by the ruins of discarded CUSN profiles. They cover the ground like confetti, and only when I wake up do I realize that I was laughing in the dream.

I'm awake at three a.m., acid reflux burning my throat and chest. I slide from bed; sweat sticks my nightgown to my skin so badly it hurts when I peel the cloth free. Joel snores. I stumble to the bathroom and swallow two antacids with tap water.

The nightmare was a new one. Dinah was guiding my hand, and I held a gun. We turned it first on Joel, then on ourselves. I suck in air, focusing on the lingering pain in my esophagus. I'm alive. Hurting is life.

No way I'll get back to sleep now. I need to know what's going to happen, and why Dinah is so certain of her predictions. I can't ask Joel. Obviously, he doesn't know what she insinuated. I don't want to upset him.

I tiptoe to the closet where I have a box of old possessions: plain glass-framed photos, my favorite college hoodie —go Badgers!—a handful of paper letters from my high school friends when we had our anachronistic phase, and an ancient laptop I modded after graduation.

It's so old that it's unregistered and disconnected from CUSN. If you flip the lid it shows a blank screen, even plugged in and battery full. I type my keycode. The screen fades into an old desktop image of my graduation class. Innocuous, even to professional eyes.

I exhale shakily. This is illegal, but what else am I supposed to do? I've always been a survivor. Pastor Snow said my resilience was God's blessing.

I connect to the net from a darkport. Joel leaves his ID badge and Behold Eden credentials on the dresser.

I'm still sore from where he dug his thumbs into my biceps while we had sex. At least he finished quick and fell asleep. Sometimes I wonder if I've forgotten what enjoyment is or if I'm just ungrateful for a husband who knows what he wants. Focus, Marely.

I adjust my CUSN profile and set it to Sleeping Peacefully. Then I dig.

It takes a few minutes to re-orient myself into the old mindset: it's uncomfortable, pretending I'm once again in my twenties, thinking I was a socialist, thinking the true order of things was wrong. Pastor Snow was firm but kind in guiding me to believe in the Truth.

But the old Marley's skills are buried there. Like riding a bike. God, I haven't seen bikes in years. I used to love my old manual Mountain Runner. I called her Cecilia.

Our household gets news from the TV, or when I occasionally glimpse shared posts from friends—usually before their husbands delete or moderate the content. I don't want to complain, but it's stifling at times, like I'm only getting the edge of a picture, the blurred pixels, not the whole image. The sudden rush of information floods my brain as I surf the legitimate feeds and then, almost by habit, slip into the grayweb info-streams.

There are those who question the stability of the economy, our country's leadership, international relations. People with low CUSN scores are in the streets in other cities, demanding work, food, medicine, rights. Riots are everywhere, according to the internet.

How is this real?

Deviants are posting their own stories—about murder and assault and imprisonment and disappearance. I can't stop reading. This isn't real. We live in America. We are safe, happy, lawful, and good.

Why are there so many lies?

Arren's name keeps being tagged. The world's inverting into a nightmare reality where nothing makes sense. We live in a world of Truth, of Purity. We are one nation under God, conservative, with Free Speech and Liberty for those who obey.

The old Marley screams somewhere in the back of my head, but I mute her. I'm not her. I'm good, I'm saved in Christ, I'm *fine*.

I narrow my searches. Looking for relevant info. I search for Behold Eden, Inc. and my skin prickles.

On the graynet, there are a hundred plus reports of Behold Eden's stocks falling, its infrastructure undermined by deviant hackers. Joel has mentioned none of this, and it's not in the approved feeds, but there is so *much* on display. The internet is full of lies, that's why we're supposed to stay in the curated and approved streams. Men of authority understand what we the people need to know; blessed by God, they keep us safe from the untruths spewed by deceivers.

The company is a leading pillar in the governmental contract neural hardware production sector, manufacturing the official CUSN and VISIONS (Virtual Inclusive Socialized and Integrated Online National Schooling) implants everyone gets at age sixteen. It's how we stay connected and safe: a chip in the back of your neck, a contact film for your eye, an audio receptacle in your ear. It's all monitored and controlled via your private interface module, the Good Citizen App. Younger generations are getting their screens embedded in their arms, though I still have to use my phone. I got a very early version of the implant and GCA. I can tamper with it, though I rarely do, because that would be unlawful and a sin, but I only consider doing that for my husband's sake. Like placing my status as Sleeping Peacefully. Maybe that's how Dinah got into my private feed. Who else might know my vulnerabilities?

Behold Eden, Inc. is losing money from faulty product, insufficient funding, and labor resistance, the lies say. Recalls are incredibly high, yet with a startlingly low follow-through. I've never seen recall announcements. Although machines produce ninety percent of the actual hardware, the wetware installation is performed by human technicians.

And there it is, buried deep, layers upon layers of untruth, the secret that makes my heart hammer: the CFO of Behold Eden was discovered to be a deviant—he's had sexual relations with another man—and now an investigation presses on to root out all the other hidden moles and corrupt employees. The conclusion: the entire workforce needs to be replaced to be certain there are no more illegals in the cogs.

This is what Dinah meant.

If Joel gets audited, he'll lose his position. And then I'll be next: my juvie record could be unveiled. Worse, my medical records will be cross-examined and—

"What the fuck are you doing?"

Joel's voice, right behind my skull. I gasp and spin.

"Nothing—"

He shoves me aside and I stumble into the counter edge. Joel's face flushes pink. He jabs a finger at the laptop screen. "What. Is. This."

I grip the marble lip, my brain stuttering. "I'm trying to protect you."

He punches me. My head rocks back. Pain and stars ricochet across my vision. For a second I can't see or hear over the echoing whirr. Shit—

"Proverbs 31:10: 'Who can find a virtuous woman? For her price is far above rubies,'" he says.

He hurls the laptop to the floor and picks up a chair. He rams the chair leg through the screen, then methodically grinds down all the broken parts. The linoleum is a map of broken glass and shattered plastic.

I gingerly touch my cheek. Skin pulses hot and swollen under my fingertips. I'll have a black eye by morning. It hurts less than the sight of my laptop shattered in pieces on the floor.

"Clean up your mess," my husband says. "I need to call Pastor Snow."

I sink to my knees and stifle a scream, and I can't tell if it's from pain or fear or rage.

I update my CUSN page after breakfast. **Tripped on my own feet and fell into the cabinet lol! Got a shiner At least I'm good at makeup! #oops #clumsyme #goodwife**

It'll delay questions at church.

My profile is a sub-page to Joel's, so I have to wait until he approves my post for the feed. Comments are easier, since they go into a queue for him to review at leisure. If I post or comment too much, he can bottleneck or cut my social access, for it's his right as the head of our household.

Joel wordlessly approves my update as he eats eggs and toast. My jaw aches so I eat oatmeal today. Immediately, a few friends react: laughing emoji, heart emoji, sadface emoji. A comment from Kitty Jansen pops up: **Haha I feel you! I tripped on the vacuum yesterday!**

I know what she really means.

After the service, Joel pulls me into Pastor Snow's private suite. I remember he once worked from an office no bigger than a walk-in closet, when he served at a tiny Baptist church in rural Wisconsin. He moved up in the world, into a national celebrity preacher. ChristTime is a megachurch. There are over five thousand people who attend in-person, and millions who watch online every Sunday morning sermons, Wednesday prayer sessions, and Saturday night worship sessions. Somehow, I never quite slipped away from his influence or presence, even though I'm nobody in comparison.

"Hi, Marley," Pastor Snow says, leaning back in his plush ergonomic chair. His glowing score—150% as befits a religious leader—halos his skull. He looks the same as he did ten years ago: his weathered face, his silver hair, his heavy jaw, his wide shoulders.

The polished glass and mahogany desk sits like an entire continent between us. "Your husband tells me there's been some problems at home."

Joel and I take our seats across from him. My tights itch my legs. The black dress at least hides sweat better than my floral-patterned cloths.

"What do you want to tell me?" Pastor Snow asks, his tone that of an elder speaking to a negligent child.

I should explain I was only trying to help Joel. But I can't mention Dinah, and she's the root of my transgression. "There's nothing wrong, Pastor Snow."

Joel's shoulders stiffen. "She was watching...porn," he grits.

I'm so shocked I nearly laugh. I cover my mouth.

"I see." Pastor Snow's disappointment echoes in his voice; he's never quiet, even when not mic'd for sermons.

"It was the deviant sort," Joel continues, and I stare at my husband, dumbfounded. "Between two *men*."

Pastor Snow grimaces. I bow my head, trying not to burst into tears from the fantastic confusion and relief. Is that what Joel thought? The last page I browsed was the report on the ex-CFO and his boyfriend. There was no nudity or visible penises anywhere. It was an old photo, one to soon crown an obituary no one will see.

"Are you unsatisfied in your marriage, Marley?" Pastor Snow asks.

The correct answer's "no." But the truth is different. My face hurts from where Joel hit me. My heart is sore from so much more than the physical pain. I don't get a chance to speak.

Joel looks away in disgust. "I provide for you, and this is your gratitude?"

Pastor Snow shakes his head. "Joel, my son, I know this is difficult. But it is a test from the Lord. We will trust in Christ to guide Marley back into the light, out of the path of sin."

It's like I'm not even *there*. A spike of anger sears through my ribs. Women aren't full citizens until married to their husbands, and that citizenship privilege can be revoked by divorce or ordinance from the Church at any time. Women exist only to support their men. It's in the Bible. I know this truth, and yet, wrong as my feelings are, I resent it.

"I've scheduled a doctor appointment for you, Marley," Pastor Snow says, his grandfatherly smile a touch sad. "My brother is the top physician in the state—you remember Frank Snow, right?"

I nod, numb. I remember Frank's hands wandered more than was professional. But he's a good man, and Pastor Snow has told me he's a good man. He's a doctor.

"We'll first make sure you are healthy and that these immoral desires are not caused by a disruption of your womanly parts."

He never could say vagina. Or vulva, clit, cervix, labia. I'm glad I had friends who taught me how to describe my body before such terms were banned. It shouldn't make me mad, but it does. Words are power, isn't that why we memorize the Bible and God's Word?

"Frank can find the cause of these…headaches." Pastor Snow's voice buzzes on.

The stress snips the stitches I sewed shut to hide my immoral, unclean thoughts years ago. Secrets pop like buttons.

A good wife is to keep no secrets from her husband. But she is also to have his best interests at heart at all times. Joel doesn't know about my high school crush on a girl, even though I did nothing about it. Not about the abortion at sixteen before the procedure was illegal. Pastor Snow wasn't famous yet. So I didn't tell him, either. Not even to ask forgiveness.

If my medical records come under scrutiny, Joel will know I had a subtotal hysterectomy and tubal ligation at twenty-one. It was black-market surgery, non-recorded. I had horrible, debilitating periods and was terrified of a full-term pregnancy and the doctor believed.

Women aren't required to get health screenings, and since I've been in good shape since marrying, I've avoided any physicals, tests, or shots. I fake my period, not that he's ever asked about the lack of bloodied tampons. Joel doesn't believe in medicine or hygienic products, not when God provides. I leave unopened tampons in restroom stalls when we go out.

My heart lurches again. Does Dinah know? Because I'll be labeled a deviant since I'm not whole. I'll be discarded.

Divorce is justified since I can't have children, but Joel might...go further.

"Okay, Marley?" asks Pastor Snow.

I snap my attention back to the office, the smell of wood polish and cologne and potpourri scenting the air to sickening levels.

"Yes, sir," I respond, and smile.

My doctor appointment is scheduled for Wednesday. Joel will take Tuesday off from work so he can "be with me in this time of strife."

I do suffer a migraine that afternoon after church. The pain slices behind my eyes, a concussive drumroll of agony through my brain. I curl up on the couch and press my face into the cushions until I pass out.

Monday.

Joel's gone by the time I wake up, and I'm shocked he let me sleep. I shower and sit at the kitchen table. There are dents in the floor where Joel slammed the chair into my laptop.

I need to keep him from uncovering my secrets. I can't take a cab without Joel's ride-code, and I'm still nauseated from the migraine. Where would I walk, anyway? There's nowhere in the city I can hide.

I pick at the incision scar at the back of my neck where the chip is lodged. There's a small micro-tattoo underneath which identifies me as Joel Leighton's wife, and the date of our marriage. Anyone who's arrested will have their tattoo run through the database and their chip scanned to make sure they are who they say.

I don't want to die in a hospital, sequestered away as one of the unfit until a permit is acquired to euthanize me. Joel told me it was cancer that killed our old neighbor, Dorothy, but I've always had my doubts. Her daughter was screaming it was state-sanctioned murder before she, too, was arrested.

I private message Dinah on CUSN. I keep it formal, so when Joel sees the queue, he won't flare up again.

Hi, Mrs. Ritter! My husband and I are excited to have dinner with you both tonight. Can I provide anything for the meal?

I have no idea if she'll see this as a plea for help, or just ignore me—I should have messaged her on the public bandwidth for such an inane query.

She replies seconds later, but the account is in her own name. Not her husband's. I'm startled. Dinah O'Fallon. **Marley, would you like to go shopping with me for dinner? I have social calls to make and would love to spend more time with you; there's nothing quite like a homecooked meal, is there? #blessed**

I lick my lips, and remember hers: lush, red, hot.

I'll need to ask Joel. He's at work until five.

How about this, Dinah replies, **I pick you up in an hour and we'll get what we need.**

It's eleven a.m. We'll have five hours. Can she help me in so short a time? My pulse thunders. To go shopping without telling Joel is a violation of our marriage contract. Although it's socially acceptable to be alone with another woman.

I can't stand being at home by myself, panicking in silence. Doing nothing's worse than acting and being punished.

I message her back: **That would be great. #letsdothis**

Dinah has her own car, which startles me more. I grip my purse, standing on the sidewalk. I chose a plain denim skirt I use to do household chores, and nice button-up blouse I inherited from my mother. It's a dove-gray, soft cotton, and it's all I have from her.

"Nice to see you, Marley," Dinah says when she rolls down the window. Her car is a sleek, black Ford sedan. The windows are tinted so dark I can't see inside. "Hop in."

I slide into the passenger seat and buckle up. Her car smells like cigarettes and cheap pine air freshener. It's immaculate otherwise: leather seats, a polished dash, but it has no CUSN radio interface.

"There are no monitors in here," Dinah says, pulling into traffic with long-practiced ease. I never got past a learner's permit. "To be specific, there are network blocks installed. We are ghosts."

I pull out my phone and sure enough, there is no signal. "How?"

"Can I trust you?" Dinah asks, never taking her gaze from the road.

"You seem to know more than I do," I reply, and I'm so desperate, I blurt out, "My husband's taking me to the doctor on Wednesday and he's going to divorce me."

Dinah nods once, a grim little head bob. "I know. The hysterectomy, right?"

I suck in my breath. "How do you—"

"I know because I know the surgeon," Dinah says. She glances at me and flashes her teeth. "Actually, she's one of my partners."

"What?"

"Listen, Marley."

I've been trying half-heartedly to pay attention to where we're driving, but I've never been good at navigating and now we're in a warehouse district and nothing is familiar. I'm not threatened by Dinah. She might be a deviant. But so what? I am too, or will be when the doctors find out.

"I'll be honest: Peter is my husband only on paper. We forged our marriage credentials ten years ago and we've been working to unmake this nightmare we live in."

"You don't have kids..." I venture, and she laughs.

"Because I'm a lesbian, yeah." She winks at me. "Peter is ace, so it works out. We're each other's cover."

It's horrifyingly treasonous and I'm in awe. They've masqueraded for ten years without being caught?

Dinah pulls into an old, empty parking lot: cracked asphalt, rusting industrial chain-link fencing, weeds sprouting between faded yellow lines. Great brick and steel buildings tower around us, shells of rust and cracked stone, boarded windows, barricaded docking doors. She parks and turns to look at me. "When my partner recognized your name in connection to Joel and Behold Eden, she asked me to help you. My question is: do you want help, Marley?"

Tears blur my eyes. I'm so tired. Of pretending I'm okay. Of simply enduring when I want to *live*.

"Yes," I say.

She reaches out and I take her hand. Her touch is warm and firm, but she's gentle—she squeezes my fingers like a friend would, not like Joel's painful grip.

"You used to be pretty good with computers, yeah?" Dinah asks.

I wipe my face and laugh bitterly. "Oh wow, that was forever ago."

"But you *can* mess with the system."

"That's how I got in this predicament," I say. "Joel caught me."

"I need your help then," Dinah says, her expression steeling. "And I'm out of time. My partner, Farah? Your old surgeon? She's been arrested."

I stiffen.

"I need you to delete Farah's profile from CUSN," Dinah

says. "So Peter and I can get her out. She'll be deported to one of the reeducation camps tomorrow." She swallows hard. The unflappable demeanor cracks: there's fear in her eyes. "I have access to a satellite office where we can get access, but I don't have the...skill." She shuts her eyes a moment. "Arren is in enough trouble, I can't ask him to risk this just now. We've got to keep him safe."

Arren made the system vulnerable. He risked everything to fight back. Dinah, too. Peter, her fake husband. I believed for so long I was a helpless, submissive woman who was only here in this world to serve the men in my life.

And what did those men ever do but cause me hurt, fear, humiliation? I used to be a rebel. I used to trust in myself. The old Marley was a fighter. I want her back.

"I'm not a believer in God," Dinah says, "but I do believe in my fellow people."

"If I can help," I say, squeezing her hand, "I'll do it."

We're nearly on the outskirts of the city. Cornfields, mostly. Huge combines towering over the crops like giant predators, ready to harvest. The fertilization system is a network of pipes and struts and massive wheels. It's like home.

Dinah cracks the window, letting in the pungent smell of corn husks and soil post-rain. It's four p.m. My feed has been dark for hours, and it's unsettling yet also calming. I never thought the silence would be so easy to enjoy. Is Joel wondering where I am? Has he alerted the police? He must have tried to contact me and gotten null pings.

What the hell am I going to do tomorrow? I have no clean clothes, no money, no phone charger—my battery's at twenty percent. Where do I sleep? How do I get my meds? I was so caught up in the rushing panic of escape I don't have a plan.

I no longer have a future, either.

"It's scary," Dinah says, as if I shared my entire private feed. "Getting out. Isn't it?"

"I don't know what happens now," I whisper.

"We get to decide that," she says. "Hold on, we're almost there. I won't abandon you, sweetheart. You won't be alone."

The endearment is too much. She isn't sarcastic or coddling. She's sincere. I start crying and can't stop. I'm not even ashamed. She has tissues in her purse and hands me a packet without taking her eyes off the road.

My face's puffy and my makeup is a runny mess when Dinah pulls into a tiny gas station off a long, winding dirt road. It looks deserted. The only hint it's not a shell is the antenna array on the roof.

"Hurry," Dinah says. She pulls a keycard from her jacket pocket and opens the dark-glass doors. I follow her inside.

It's no AmeriCo—instead, there are rows and rows of

terminals, all dark and dusty, with ropey tangles of cabling pulled through exposed I-beams in the ceiling.

"This is a station we liberated awhile back," Dinah says, guiding me by the elbow. She points to a massive virtual reality chair in the corner: one of the early VISIONS hubs. "That's an admin port," she says. "You can access everything. You have to act fast, Marley. Please. There's not much time. New processes deport at seven p.m., and Peter has a crew standing by for my signal."

Her hand is sweaty, damp even through my shirt. I swallow hard and nod. "Give me her ID."

She does.

I haven't been inside an actual VISIONS hub in years, but I remember the interface well. I slide into the haptic-sensor seat, pull down the visor, and extend the keyboard control wings over my lap. With a deep breath, I lean my head back and let the port sync into my chip.

Then I'm inside CUSN's world.

This VISIONS hub's virtual reality model looks like a small Baptist church building in rural Wisconsin. I realize that my old profile setup is still patterned in my chip, so this is what my "home base" would look like. It's claustrophobic. I want to bust through the narrow windows and flee into the prairie.

It's not real, Marley. This is an overlay. You aren't going back.

The simulation maps the databases onto the pages of a great bible on the pulpit. I stand at the lectern, a sudden wave of nausea rocking me. Information floods across my awareness: I really am an admin. Before, if I looked at this unreal Bible, I would only have seen scripture.

Now I see code.

I enter Farah Mendez's ID. She appears in a pew near the rear of the worship hall: gray slicks her temples, her dark hair caught back in a severe bun. Dark circles bruise her eyes. She looks exhausted.

Then the program begins to auto-populate based on my ID. Friends from the city. People from church.

Pastor Snow and my husband sit in the front pew. This is a simulation, but I'm observing their uplinked interfaces: if I show myself to them, they'll see. I can connect through the webbed networks and come back online. They might not be able to locate me right away, unless I give coordinates, but they will know it's me. Through Pastor Snow, I can reach the entire congregation's networks, the way he sends out weekly prayer reminders.

Panic tightens my chest. Because now there are police, and Joel's coworkers, and I recognize his boss. They are all crowded into the pews, expressions a mural of anger, disgust, suspicion.

Peter Ritter blinks into view near the worship hall doors. He's in black riot gear. Phantasm shapes—his team?—blur just out of focus around him. Dinah isn't here, because like me, she's off-grid. I bet the old gas station has a modified null-field that blocks uplink signal.

I tap into Pastor Snow's sphere, and suddenly I can hear everything going on: he and Joel are at our condo, with the police, with representatives from Behold Eden, Inc. Joel has been fired, and everyone demands to know where I am.

"I've done nothing wrong!" Joel yells.

Pastor Snow's voice is bereft of comfort. "You aided and abetted a known terrorist."

"I don't even know this deviant Arren. I'm a lawful citizen, I'm not a sinner. You know me, sir."

"Everyone at Behold Eden has been compromised," Pastor Snow continues. As the leader of ChristTime, he has both religious authority and governmental sway. It's a politically sound move for him to be the one who uproots the sin and turns in his wayward flock. A shepherd must protect the greater good, and some sheep will always be led to the slaughter. "If you cooperate and tell us where Marley is, I will pray to God to forgive you for this heinous crime."

I'm the one at the pulpit, and this is my congregation.

I could save Joel. I could take the blame, tell everyone I was the mole, that he's an innocent man. It's what he would expect of me if he knew. I imagine Pastor Snow's voice: *It is God's will for you, daughter. You must prove your faith. Even though you perish, your husband may live.*

My hand shakes. Ultimate redemption—isn't that what

the Bible says? Laying down your life for your husband? Eternal glory in the arms of God awaits the penitent.

I have served, I have strived, I have starved myself into a shadow of who I am. I look at Farah, weary and alone, condemned for helping the downtrodden. She never asked for payment when I sought her out, desperate to prevent a future of being tethered to all the children I was expected to have. She worked for a black-market clinic, once a Planned Parenthood, and she never asked me to justify my choice.

How many other people has she saved, tirelessly, even though it costs her everything? She deserves better. We all do.

I can't give any more. And I don't *want* to give.

No more.

The rage I've buttoned down for years comes roaring back like a banshee, a siren, a witch's scream.

Fuck this world.

I don't owe my life and my happiness to a man who hurts me. I don't owe the church shit—for what has it ever brought but pain and humiliation? Fuck you, Pastor Snow, and your idea of God. Fuck this system and all its corrupt, hypocritical sycophants.

FUCK IT ALL.

I pull Farah Mendez's Genesis Code—the root of every profile—from the tangled layers of protection and observation. There are years of governmental tags, citations, warnings, fines. I hold the Genesis Code in my hand, then I delete it. Farah disappears. I send a message to Peter: **Farah is out of the system. Dinah's safe with me.**

He twitches, but he's ex-military, and he's professional. **Thanks.**

Then he's moving, bursting out the doors of the worship hall—in reality, I don't know where he is. I don't want to compromise him.

Pastor Snow and Joel are shouting at each other. I hear my name. I will not answer.

My life is my own now. And I am not going back.

I delete my Genesis Code from the system; my profile goes dark.

Joel is on his own.

I blink as the visor scrolls back into its dock and I'm back in the physical, non-VISIONS world. The itch in the back of my neck has become a burning pain. I've fried my chip with the last deletion. It hurts, but it won't kill me. Not anymore.

I look up, and Dinah stops pacing.

"Farah's profile is ghosted," I say. "I told Peter. He'll free her."

Dinah exhales, blinking hard, and nods. "Thank you, Marley."

I gingerly slid out of the chair, my legs unsteady. She offers an arm to support me.

"I'm also gone," I tell her, and wince as the blisters on my neck throb. "I can't do that again, I'm afraid."

"It's okay," she says. "There are others who can. You bought us time."

I nod, trembling harder. Time. Future. What does it look like on this side of the glass?

"There are a million more like us," Dinah says. "It's going to be slow and hard, but we can help them. I can't do it alone."

"You're not alone," I say. She draws me close. Her breath is like the breeze of paradise.

She kisses me, and my brain surges with revelation and relief and yearning and excitement and hope. I understand how lost I was before until she found me.

"Let's go," Dinah says. "I want to reintroduce you to Farah."

I nod, giddy. She's real, she's alive, and so am I. We are the future.

"Yes," I say. "Let's burn this system down."

THE
LAW
IS THE
PLAN,
AND THE
PLAN IS
DEATH

THE LAW IS THE PLAN, AND THE PLAN IS DEATH

"We must all obey the great law of change. It is the most powerful law of nature."

EDMUND BURKE

The world is ending one deleted profile at a time and there's nothing you can do about it. Just as you're about to fine an account for taking the Lord's name in vain, it vanishes with an error message: PROFILE NOT FOUND. You rub your eyes, the screens blaring content into your brain at warp speed. You've already been working for six hours, and you've barely scratched the surface of your queue.

Worst of it is, each deletion is a mark against your account, and your score is dipping dangerously towards the mid-eighties.

In the six months since the apocalyptic data breach instigated by the terrorist group Unchained, you've barely slept more than five hours a night, pulling double and sometimes triple shifts to tourniquet the damage. You job is monitoring questionable material and ensuring that uploaded content to CUSN profiles is Lawful and Good. It used to be easy: a couple hundred posts a day, monitored and tagged. Citizen's United Social Networking's Midwest Headquarters was a decent place to work until the massive, viral attack on America's foundational social networks happened. The hack let people mutate their profiles—changing biological truths like sex and gender markers, names, or even sexual orientation—or disappear entirely. It's ludicrous, absolute, pure treason and sin. Brilliant on a technological level, you gotta admit, but that's an opinion that will get you arrested.

The rules have changed. Instead of penalizing accounts with social score fines or governmental disapproval markers, you're authorized to outright criminalize anyone who modifies their profile against their State-appointed identification data. Before the hack, this kind of power would be terrifying and restricted to managerial level overseers only. But both your sector leads vanished. And it was just last week that a disgruntled security guard broke in (on your only day off, fucking hell, thank the Lord) and shot up the floor stations, killing seventy-five coworkers.

It was his right to express his free speech and carry an automatic rifle. You've got to remember that. He was a white Christian man and his social score was at 87%. On the cam footage, you heard his statement that due to the hack, his wife had become a lesbian, deleted her profile, and run away, taking their five-year-old son with her. He was arrested, unharmed of course, and aside from property damage fines, he won't face criminal charges. He's an upstanding member of the Church and the community.

But there are still bloodstains on nearby station monitors and every time the doors creak or someone coughs, you jump, your pulse ricocheting between your throat and ears.

You don't have the luxury of a break. Your bladder is full and your stomach hurts from the bitter cafeteria coffee, but you only have two bathroom passes on your employee ID for the rest of the day. Three coworkers didn't show up for shifts, which leaves you to pick up the slack.

You haven't quite had the nerve to see if their profiles have vanished, or if they are simply jailed or dead. Best not to wonder about it. It's unproductive.

The cubicle is hot, the air stifling, and the little USB powered desk fan does squat to cool you down. Sweat itches your neck, makes your polo cling to your armpits. Deodorant is a long-lost memory by 10a.m.

Your CUSN wristband buzzes. Your supervisor, Isaac, wants to see you. You wipe your face, your blood pressure rising. This is going to further indent your scores, because there's no one to cover your console—and Isaac likes to chat, so it's not going to be quick. Dammit.

Refusal will just get you a fine for disrespect, so you set your status to Supervisory Pause—even that will go to Isaac for approval, and dear lord, you hope he doesn't delay because otherwise you'll be fined for misuse of authority status—and jog towards the elevator. Your bladder is about to stage rebellion.

Isaac's office is cramped, bright with fluorescent lights, and has one pane of bullet-proof glass overlooking the cubicles on the first floor. Isaac hunches over his desk, deep circles under his eyes, his hair a greasy tangle, his uniform rumpled.

"Eleazar," Isaac says, and waves at a rolling chair piled with paper take-out containers. "I'll keep this brief."

You gingerly nudge the trash into the bin beside the desk and sit, wishing you could fish out a plastic bottle and piss in it just to relieve the pain. Isaac is never brief.

Before the hack, you would arrive every day at work and settle into your appointed workstation. Triple screens scrolled streams of content: posts, updates, videos, photos, VR exports. Almost on autopilot, you would flag anything with potential deviant messages. Women friends standing too close together could be misinterpreted, so the photo must be deleted and the CUSN users fined. A post that failed to capitalize God would be edited and allowed, but a fine must follow. Then there were the insidious, subtler posts that tried to bury subtext and messages within genial wording. Those were harder to pin down, but you have a knack for this: you can read between the lines, as it were. That's why you had such an outstanding employee score of 96% accuracy.

Now, when you can't keep up with the vanishing profiles, each missed post or mistake costs you points. Your rating blares in dark orange at the corner of your eye: 86%. At eighty-five you'll be called in for an evaluative meeting. If your score ever drops below eighty, you're fired. Without a good job, you'll lose credit, and without credit obviously your rent goes up triple the cost, which of course you can't afford, and a cascade of other effects pile on until you're broke, homeless, ostracized from former social circles, and a step away from debtors jail, where it's impossible to pay back the loans you've got no choice but to accept. Non-compliance means your citizenship is revoked, and once *that* happens, you're basically as good as dead.

"This is my last day," Isaac says, and your brain sluggishly tries to process that because what the fuck? Isaac is a staggering 98% in managerial scores, he has amazing social credit, and until a week ago you thought he unironically loved his job here.

"You're transferring?" you ask, because that's the only thing that makes sense.

Isaac laughs, and it's a frighteningly bleak sound. "Fuck no."

"I don't understand, sir."

He suddenly shoves his monitor, coffee mug, photos of

his wife Monica, and a stack of paperwork off the desk with one dramatic sweep of his arm, like he's a gif come to life. "I'm done," Isaac says. He throws something at you, and you flinch back. The chair rolls you towards the door.

His access card clatters to the floor in front of you.

"It's open," Isaac says. "Hacked."

"What?" It hurts to bend down, but you scoop up the plastic ID and stare at it. The faint holographic imprints glimmer: Isaac's supervisor credentials, the blaring CUSN logo, the privilege level embossed over his photo: Class A.

"I can't do this anymore," Isaac says, and you finally notice the booze on his breath, over the stale smells of body odor and uncirculated air and old freedom fries. He unholsters his pistol and lays it on the desk, and your heart skips, is he going to murder you—

"I'm not gonna shoot you," Isaac says, like that'll do shit all to calm you down.

It's mandatory for all male citizens, if white, to own a gun. To know how to use it. You trained in the virtual reality VISIONS platform, as part of your life score and credit rating. But since the shooting, cubicle employees are required to store their firearms in a locker before entering the premises. Managers excluded.

"I d-don't understand, sir." You swallow hard. *Don't piss yourself,* is about the only clear thought you can hang onto. Maybe you have good reason now, with the semi-automatic's barrel pointed in your direction, but it'd be fucking embarrassing and you don't have a change of pants available.

"Monica's gone," Isaac says. "Citizen arrest malfunction, is the—that's what the police call it. Our neighbor..." He scrubs his face with both hands, his voice shaking. "Well, he thought she was a deviant. Caught her 'looking lustfully' at his own wife and..."

Oh, fuck. You know where this is going and there's damned all you can do.

"So he shot her," Isaac says, and it's worse that he isn't crying, that he *can't*. "Right in our front yard. While I was here. It was...it was two days ago."

He wasn't in yesterday, but you thought it was just his rest period. "Shit, I'm sorry..."

Isaac shakes his head viciously. "Don't. Just don't, man."

Whenever people call you man, or "sir" you, or call you mister, it feels like a spider bite. Itchy, a little bit painful, but nothing you can do about it. Spider is long gone, and all that you have to show for it is a tiny welt.

"I can cover the floor," you offer, and it sounds as mediocre and useless as it is. What else can you do? You can't keep up with your own queue and now Isaac is a wreck and you're holding his damned ID badge that he said was open. Hacked? What the hell for?

"You could do more than that, Eleazar." Isaac spins the pistol around, his index finger in the trigger guard, and you stiffen. You have no idea if he has the safety on.

You open your mouth, but words are blank holes and you're getting dizzy. The air is too close in here. You can't stop looking at the gun.

"You know, there was this dude who once said, 'The only thing necessary for the triumph of evil is for good men to do nothing.' Or something like that. But he's full of shit." Isaac spits to the side, his eyes bloodshot. "There are no good men. Not in positions of power, not anywhere. But there are men who do nothing, so evil triumphs all the same."

"I really got to get back to work," you stammer, but Isaac shakes his head again.

"Listen, Eleazar." Isaac lays his palm on the pistol butt. The barrel faces the window now.

You swallow hard. You don't want to die here in this stuffy little office with an unused bathroom break on your ID badge and a legacy of nothing. Who are you, really? Just another person crushed under the daily grind, panicking about paying bills and keeping your scores up and waking in cold sweats when you dream about dying in your cubicle with a bullet through your brain.

It's weird because as a kid, you had these ambitions, these wild dreams that when you grew up, you'd *do* something worthwhile. You'd be an astronaut or an Olympic medalist or a famous doctor who saved lives every day. You got older, and more jaded, and you narrowed your dreams. Maybe you'd just be in a stable job, have a family, own a nice house if you won the lottery in credit score and investment financing.

Now you just want to survive to go home in ten hours and sleep hard enough to forget everything before you repeat it all tomorrow.

"I knew Arren Darden," Isaac says quietly. "I helped him...I helped him with the breach."

What. The. Fuck?

Isaac lets out a bitter laugh. "I thought we'd get away with it, too. But I got scared once shit hit the fan. I was scared Monica would—" He chokes, fights for breath, and forces himself onward. "That we'd be caught and punished. So I burned the contacts. Offered a scapegoat. Pretended I knew nothing."

And now his wife is dead for some excuse by a jealous neighbor, and there will be a detailed evaluation of Isaac's personal life because of the accusation of deviance. Someone will find something, and he'll be screwed. He probably already is, because the safety monitoring system in the building will be recording all this and when the logs are reviewed by the automated propriety screeners, he'll be dead.

"This is wrong." The words burst out of you before you can stop them. The system, the punishments, the grinding despair that you all endure day after day. "This is all bullshit!"

Isaac shrugs. "Yeah." All the verve has drained from him; he looks like a walking corpse, sallow and dead-eyed and listless. "You better get back to work." He lifts the pistol and puts the muzzle under his chin. "Maybe you can do better."

You jerk up from the chair, stumble over trash, and jam your elbow painfully into the door before you manage to twist the handle. You slam the door shut behind you and it doesn't muffle the gunshot.

You've still got Isaac's ID in your hand.

You use his pass to get into the men's bathroom and finally pee, and it's such a pained relief you realize halfway through you're crying, shaking, and feel sick. You brace your arms against the wall on either side of the toilet, glad you found a stall so you could lock the door for minimal privacy.

Shit, shit, *shit*.

Isaac is dead. There will be an investigation soon, and you might be implicated for hearing treason. It's been fifteen minutes since you left your workstation, and you practically feel your score nosediving. Isaac never approved the break. His ID card burns in your pocket; it might not be blood-stained but you hate touching it all the same.

You need to focus. Head down, take the day one step at a time. You have his credentials. You could back-date the authorization. Most workplace suicides are rarely time-stamped unless it affects profit, but with the chaos of the breach and the recent shooting, you might be able to fudge things enough to avoid a penalty.

It's disgusting how rational your thoughts are right now. You liked Isaac. He was a decent guy, and he did his best to vouch for his employees. He pulled longer hours than he needed to try and help with the backlog. He didn't deserve this.

You wash your hands and flee back to your cubicle. It's

like a ghost town on the floor now. The few people who clocked in have vanished. They must have heard the gunshot and decided to take the fine for abandoning a shift rather than risk dying. You can't blame anyone. If you didn't have his ID in your possession, you'd be tempted to flee, too. It's never been so quiet in here.

There's no one here to report you. Your hands are still trembling as you swipe Isaac's card in the login terminal on the console next to yours. It belongs—belonged, dammit—to Stacey, one of the casualties in the shooting. You try to ignore the mug with WORLD'S TOP MOM filled with popsicle stick artwork from her kids that sits beside the monitor.

The supervisor interface is similar to yours when you open your queue: only there are side menus with additional dropdowns for employee management, admin tasks, disciplinary action, and time-card review.

Maybe you can do better.

What can you do, one lone worker against the uncaring fist of government and centuries of unchallenged power? You could avoid being fired, at least today. It's a small thing in the grand cosmic scale, or the eyes of God. But it's your choice. It's radical to save yourself when no one else will.

You type in your employee number and give yourself an extended grace period for priority managerial meetings. Your time clock score tweaks back into the green. You breathe out in relief. It's so quiet on the floor your heart-beat is like a broken kick drum. You're too exposed here, and you wish for privacy, but going into Isaac's office is worse.

There's a spam-like link at the top of Isaac's dashboard which catches your eye. Ugly blue text directing to 'open source liberty.' No one is around to stop you. You click, and a secondary dashboard pops up, and you cringe, expecting porn or a virus alert to fill the screen. Instead, the new screen has additional drop-down menus for deepadmin functions: adjustments to individuals' social credit scores, life statuses, and profile creation/deletion. You nervously navigate through a few more nested menus and catch your breath in shock.

You stare for a long moment, trying to process the sheer power you hold: somehow, Isaac has access to the virtual mainframe of Citizen's United Social Networking. It's like staring into the matrix of life itself. This is like the damn nuclear codes.

From this dinky console in a ghost town office, you can change the fate of millions of American citizens with a few command prompts. This is a macro version of what the breach did for individual users, but instead of changing your personal account, you could change...everyone's.

And Isaac is dead and can't be penalized for what you do.

Why did he burden you with this? Was it just because you were there, toiling away, trying to do your best to get by? Did he know something about you that you don't?

When you were a kid, before it was banned, you remember reading an illegal paperback copy of *Lord of the*

Rings and you feel a bit like Frodo at the moment. Standing in Mordor, tired and hungry and scared, and Mount Doom is still miles away.

You've heard rumors that in other countries, there is no equivalent of CUSN, that there are free internets and people who thrive online and off, unafraid to be who they are. Is that possible? It's such a wild idea, like the fantasy bullshit you used to love.

A chat bubble pops open, sender unknown. **Isaac, what are you doing?**

You jump. Ignore it, the smarter part of your brain warns. Better yet, smash the console and get the fuck out.

Which is pointless, because there are already logs of you working, talking to Isaac before his death, and you realize with a stomach-turning lurch the security feeds will have seen you hacking an unused console.

You're screwed. There's no running and no hiding for you now.

I'm not Isaac. He's dead.

A half second leg. Then:

Oh. Damn. Who's this?

Does it matter how much you say or withhold? It's probably a federal agent on the other end of the chat. It's not like that matters now. Having anyone to talk to is all that's holding you together.

I'm Eleazar. Isaac...he killed himself. Just now.

The gunshot still rings in your ears, or maybe that's just phantom memory and shock.

Shit. I'm sorry.

Sorry? Why? Is this a ploy for camaraderie or—fuck, your vision blurs again and you hastily wipe your eyes.

Who're you? you type back, with more force than the keyboard deserves.

I'm Peter Ritter. A friend.

Just walk away. Unplug the console, logout of your idling station—now building up penalties for non-useful time spent—and...what?

You can't go home. If the police are not already on their way they will be soon. You'll be arrested. Fined, jailed, then executed because fuck if there is any pilot in a trial for a lawbreaker like you.

You're too late to help your friend, you retort, and the keyboard shudders under your anger.

The text chat suddenly morphs into video, and *shit*, you realize you never turned Stacey's GEM off. Way to go. The Good Employee Monitor is a sleek little webcam built into the cubicle to track progress and interface with company webinars or mandatory live training sessions, which always take place during work hours and CUSN technicians are expected to maintain their workload and progress while attending virtual trainings.

You flinch back from the screen as the video window displays Peter Ritter's face. Or who you assume is the man from the chat. He's white, handsome, with a neatly trimmed brown beard and kind eyes. He wears camouflage fatigues. Military.

"I'm Pete," he says. "I'm sorry to hear...about Isaac."

You nod, unsure what else to do.

"Listen." Pete squints, his gaze flicking behind you, and you realize he's trying to see what else is around. "You have admin access to the building if you're in Isaac's account," Pete says. "I recommend locking the exterior doors and putting the workstations into lockdown."

"Why?" It's a stupid question and you know the answer immediately, even though Pete replies with the same calm, professional manner.

"A suppression unit is on its way to your location."

Your skin crawls and a chill dances down your back. Fuck. A police suppression unit has only one task: total elimination of hostiles within a government-owned building. Which is now just you, probably.

It's surprisingly easy from Isaac's account to engage emergency defense systems.

The heavy bullet-proof shutters glide down over the doors, and distantly you hear the grinding of locks and shielding snapping into place over exits and windows. Anti-terrorist protective measures. They never would have been triggered for the shooter a week ago, even if Isaac had been in his office to manually activate the defenses: the shooter's privilege scores were too high.

"Good job," Pete says. "CUSN buildings have top-notch defense grids. You'll be safe for the time being, okay?"

Safe? The word is laughable. How can you ever be safe again?

"I don't know what to do," you whisper, and sink onto the chair. It still smells like Stacey's perfume: lilacs and carnations. Everything is so goddamn overwhelming you want to curl up in a fetal position or scream. Maybe both. Instead, you stare dully at the monitor.

"Let us help you."

"Who's 'us'?" You choke on a bitter laugh. "You can't help me. I'm alone."

"No, you're not."

Pete shifts his position and another face leans into view. A younger man than Pete—also white—he's chubby and short, dressed in a loose dress shirt with the sleeves rolled up and cargo shorts. His hair is tousled, he wears metal studs in his ears and a septum ring, and what looks like the edge of a tattoo peeks up over his collarbone.

"Hey, I'm Arren Darden."

What the *fuck*?

And then another person: a woman with brown skin and black hair pinned up in a bun, wearing blue medical scrubs and a white jacket. Her mascara is immaculate, and she wears a silver necklace with a cross on it.

"Hello, Eleazar, I'm Doctor Farah."

They crowd close to Pete, lit by the screen, everyone looking at you with earnest...compassion? This is so much to process, and your brain is overtaxed as it is.

"I have my squad on their way to intercept the suppression unit," Pete says. "You hold on, okay?"

"We're rebels, according to the government," Doctor

Farah says with a wry smile. She has a slight foreign accent, which startles you. The Midwest HQ is so homogenized you sometimes forget not everyone has the same manner of speech as you and Isaac and Stacey and...all the rest. "Does not mean we are not well-prepared or capable of resistance."

You nod, numb. It's too much to try and hope Pete's people will get to you before the police do. You can't even get into Isaac's office anymore, because of the lockdown. So you've got no weapons and no chance.

"Hey, Eleazar?"

It's Arren. He looks a lot younger than you expected for being the nation's most wanted terrorist. He's got sleep-debt bags under his eyes and the tiniest bit of stubble on his upper lip and jaw, but otherwise his features are smooth. His voice is nasally and low, and you have to admit that he doesn't look like the deviant boogeyman you'd always pictured when you heard his name before.

"It's okay if you're scared," Arren says. "Hell, that's me all the time. I know you don't know us, but we're not gonna abandon you, okay? Pete's guys are all former marines. They know what they're doing and they're gonna help you."

"They assisted in my release from prison," Doctor Farrah adds. "They are good people, as are you."

Your throat feels too thick to respond, so you nod again.

Rumbling outside. Vehicles. Air support. You hunch your shoulders. You want to crawl under Stacey's desk, but it'd be pointless, and then you couldn't see Pete and Arren and Doctor Farah. It'd be so easy for them to just snip the connection, go find someone else to save. You don't want to die, and you doubt they want to *watch* you die, but here they are, still online with you.

You eye the second monitor, where the admin screen remains open and full of terrible possibility.

"You initiated the breach," you mumble, glancing sidelong at Arren. "Why stop there?"

Arren smiles slightly. "It's hard when you're always on the run. I can't get past the firewalls. That's why I need..." He hesitates, swallows. "Needed Isaac's help. And now yours, I guess? If—if you want. You're *in* CUSN. It's all open from your end."

Maybe you can do better.

The facility has secondary and tertiary backup generators and power supplies, so unless the suppression unit nukes the whole grid, buildings and all, you won't lose connection for a while. It'll take the police less time to bulldoze one of the outside walls and storm the floor and kill you than it will to cut off your power and access to the networks.

For a moment, you entertain the idea of just sitting tight and waiting for the police to arrive. You have evidence, right? You could prove you lured out the mastermind of the breach—Arren fucking Draden—and his cohorts. Someone could trace the call, given the deepadmin privileges. If this was a movie, you'd be a hacker, working to trace the location of Arren, Farah, and Pete, ready to sic an elite suppression unit on them while they think they have you cornered. Smashcut to the rebel base being invaded, the leaders shot in a hyperreal series of shots, blood spraying the camera. Back to CUSN HQ, where you're shaking hands with the SWAT leader, triumphant music plays, and a montage begins: you at the press conference, accepting a medal of honor, everyone cheering your name.

Nice fantasy, right?

Reality is a cold, nasty bitch. Because you *know* what'll happen the moment the suppression unit gets through the defenses. You're compromised. You'll be lucky if you aren't sniped—or maybe luck is not seeing it coming, just a sudden headshot that doesn't leave time for terror. Perhaps you'll be exonerated posthumously; you might be a footnote of some government report, a harried agent noting that you *tried* to do the right then, even if it was too late. That's a stretch. No one will care that you tried to back-trace Arren's location. Or someone else will take the credit for it.

No, the fact is, unless Pete's people get here fast, you're gonna die. It won't be clean.

Your friends will be fed propaganda about terrorist attacks that led to your death, and your possessions will be seized by the state, and your credit ratings will be zeroed so no next of kin—your estranged sister, your uncle whom you haven't seen in ten years, and fuck, there isn't anyone else, is there?—can't claim any death benefits. Friends and coworkers will shake their heads, wondering how they didn't see it coming.

He was always so quiet and hard-working, people will say, judging you for being the monster at the end of the book. Even thinking about how much your name and he/him/his will be bandied about makes you cringe inwardly.

They! you want to shout at the world, a crashing realization flooding your brain. Because holy shit. There's a word for you, isn't there? A pronoun. An identity. A you. *They/them.*

Maybe it's the adrenaline or the terror or thirty years of feeling uncomfortable in your skin, but the paradigm shift makes you suddenly dizzy. You grip the desk edge, blinking hard. They. Them. You aren't a he, and it's been a long time since you felt like that was true.

Holy goddamn fucking shit—there's a word for who you *are*. Nothing like foxhole conversion, or more like foxhole acceptance.

"Eleazar?" Arren asks, his brows knitted in worry.

"You okay, man?" Pete asks, leaning towards the camera.

"I'm not a he," you say, your voice shaking. You look at the three strangers, these witnesses to your truth. "I'm a they."

"Ah, you are non-binary?" Doctor Farah smiles kindly. "It is good to know."

Your whole body flushes hot and cold and you shiver like you're about to get sick but it's this weird, cramping, terrifying elation.

"Deep breaths," Doctor Farah adds, and she's so kind about it—what's wild is none of the three are the slightest bit fazed. They look...happy? Like they're glad you've figured out this life-changing revelation that feels so true, even though it's minutes before you're gonna die?

"It's a trip, isn't it?" Arren flashes you a tired grin. "When I figured out I was trans, it was a hell of a relief, let me tell you."

You nod, your thoughts still spinning.

"Not to be that asshole to rain on the parade, folks, but Eleazar is in danger," Pete says. He glances at Arren and Doctor Farah. "We gotta buy them time. My guys are still en route."

An electric thrill tap-dances along your spine. *Buy them time.* Them. You. Is this what euphoria is like, sans drugs or sex? Or is that your brain passing from animalistic terror into a serene fuck-the-system-we-don't-give-a-shit-anymore defiance? Either way, you like it. It's better than the gut-churning dread.

Arren sobers, pressing his face close so he fills most of the screen. "Okay, listen to me."

You suck in a huge lungful of stale air and hold onto the desk's edge for support, as if the chair will vaporize under you and plant you on your ass. Your hands sweat and your mouth is so dry it hurts. Strident, wailing sirens creep through the lockdown. You don't have long.

"We can delete your profile," Arren is saying. "That will mostly help protect anyone you know from immediate back-lash, since it fucks up the algorithms and—"

"I want to delete it all," you tell him. Adrenaline lights up your whole body. Like an action hero in a movie, taking a last stand, you have a chance to change everything—though you'll die trying. "Delete the whole system."

Arren's mouth hangs open and he blinks. Pete whistles. Doctor Farah smiles slowly, a gleam in her dark eyes.

"I like the way they think," Doctor Farah says. She nudges Arren with her elbow. "Isn't this what we've been trying to do? A full shut-down?"

"Yeah..." Arren blinks rapidly, and you can imagine his thoughts racing, a plan formulating in his brain.

"I'm out of time," you say, and your voice is eerily steady. "I've got one shot. Tell me how to burn this goddamn system down."

America was built on revolution, on bloodshed, on chaos. What's one more rebirth in the reincarnation of a country?

If you delete CUSN, removing all profiles, eliminating every citizen's social scores—it'll be anarchy. Every person would be equal for a moment, like in death. Pastors and politicians, factory workers and farmers, CEOs and commoners. Everyone would be the same: zero.

The ripple effect will cascade through financial sectors; job markets will crash; crime will explode as no one can be tracked for civil infractions; deviants can't be prosecuted; the powerful will fear the powerless again. In the few hours or days or weeks to come, the people will rise.

"Okay," Arren says, and he begins to talk you through the interface, the backdoors into the whole system.

You want to believe things will change. They have in the

past, right? If CUSN could evolve over your life, if you can still remember when there was possibility to *live*, when you could imagine a future, then that time can come again. You might not see it. But others will.

Sweat drips into your eyes. Warnings and alerts flare on the screen, but you ignore them. Arren's voice is suddenly accompanied by the first few notes of a song, one you vaguely remember hearing long ago. The music is faint, tinny from being played on cheap speakers, and Arren fishes out an ancient phone from his pocket. A ringtone. A gravelly voice half-whispers, "Hello darkness, my old friend..."

Pete takes the phone from Arren and flips it open. The music clips off, but the melody is in your head now.

"Marley and Dinah are on their way," Pete says to Doctor Farah, and he stands. He looks at you, even though your focus is ratcheted into the deepadmin pages, and it takes all your concentration to follow Arren's directions and keep up.

"Hold fast, Eleazar," Pete says. "We won't abandon you."

You believe him. Regardless of what happens, you aren't alone.

You remember bits of the lyric to Arren's ringtone song, heard so long ago. "...disturb the sound of silence."

You will.

There it is, finally: the metaphorical keys to the mother-fucking kingdom. With a few keystrokes, you can delete everything. Bring CUSN down. Black out the social scoring and credit system.

"That's it," Arren says, biting his cuticles. He looks terrified, when you feel bizarrely calm. The sound of metal-cutters being used on the outside shields seeps through the barriers. The suppression unit is here. "We might lose connection when you do this. Once the networks go down..."

"I'm okay," you tell him. Whatever happens after this, it can't be undone. Isaac thought you could do better, and you have. You're at peace with that. You know who you are and what you want.

A better tomorrow.

You delete the core. All around the floor stations, monitors flare with error pages. The chat window vanishes, but you know Arren and Doctor Farah and Pete are still on the other end, somewhere. You remove Isaac's card and tuck it in your pocket.

The suppression unit stops its forced entry and the sirens go quiet. Probably frazzled from the sudden loss of info or contact. Or Pete's marines have arrived.

You shut down the console and begin walking to each cubicle and unplugging the computers. One by one, the lights of screens go dark, just like all over the country, digital infrastructures are dying.

When the last computer is shut down, when only the emergency lights illuminate the floor, you sit down by your station and wait.

The world has ended because of what you've done. A new one will begin, soon, and this one will be better.

THANK
YOU FOR
YOUR
PARTICIPATION
IN THIS
MANDATORY
SATISFACTION
SURVEY

THANK YOU FOR YOUR PARTICIPATION IN THIS MANDATORY SATISFACTION SURVEY

Welcome, Madison Roberts! Thank you for filling out your Annual Citizen's Satisfaction Survey in a timely manner. Please answer all questions to the best of your ability and remember that unacceptable responses will be subject to audited review, for your own safety and happiness.

1.) On a scale of 1-10, how satisfied are you with your assigned role in society?

Ten. My role as stay-at-home mom and managing my husband's household is fulfilling. I am able to clean fastidiously, cook good meals for my hard-working husband, care for my two children, and maintain my physically appealing demeanor, in accordance with local bylines. I always have time to go to the hardware store, stop by the local market, and otherwise run errands. My husband now owns a brand-new gas mask for when he practices his airbrushing! I wouldn't want him to inhale any fumes while enjoying his hobby. I listen attentively whenever he speaks and always praise his opinions, as a dutiful wife should. I would never consider contradicting my husband's views, or teaching my children to lie to him. Children must be taught the truth.

2.) On a scale of 1-10, how satisfied are you with the statutes of the Law and Abiding Principles that govern our country?

Ten. I believe in the value our Laws and how this has made our country great. We are free of unlawful aliens, alternative behaviors, and no longer need fear for our safety of unmoderated social media. All is seen, so all is safe!

3.) As a Citizen, how would you classify your patriotic engagement with sanctioned actives (such as the Daily Pledge, viewing The Citizen's Eye program, and fulfillment of the Watch Thy Neighbor reports)? Rate on a scale 1-10.

Ten. I'm a loyal and punctual reporter for the Watch Thy Neighbor program. Fortunately for us all, my neighbors are upstanding, perfect citizens who have done no wrong! We often gather at each other's houses in the evenings to praise the Lawful State and share our mutual love of the Lawful Police and our government.

4.) *How often do you participate in the State Church's weekly services?*

My husband faithfully attends services every weekend, along with our children, and myself. I would never consider missing a service in order to meet friends or plan extracurricular activities. Holy days, when governmental buildings are closed in reverence to the State Church, are for rest and worship. Of course I would report any suspicious activity such as trespassing.

5.) *On a scale of 1-10, how would you rate your opinion of the Lawful State Police?*

Ten. The Lawful State Police is above reproach. The detainment and disappearance of my twin sister last month was absolutely necessary, and I have never mourned her, as she was a traitor who sought to disobey the government. While the blueprints to the Lawful State Police HQ and the chemical airborne toxins were never found, I have absolute faith they are of no longer any danger to upstanding citizens such as myself.

. . .

6.) You are registered as being in sanctioned, lawful marriage to Mr. Dennis Roberts. On a scale of 1-10, how would you rate your fulfillment in your wifely duties to Mr. Roberts, as described under Statute 178.4 of the Lawful Coupling Act?

Ten. My husband is an ideal man, whom I love as is proper. I and my children are honored that he works for the Lawful Police in the HQ building. While it is true he was one of the arresting officers of my sister, how can I do anything but love him for following his duty?

7.) Finally, on a scale of 1-10, do you consider yourself to have any Defects, inherited or recently acquired, as defined under the Citizen Pedigree Statutes 56.1E?

One, since I can't rate myself zero. My husband often compliments me on my high intelligence, and my skill with tools. While it is true my twin sister was a skilled chemist and was alleged to have used her knowledge to plant biohazard nodules in government buildings, even if she was arrested before she could trigger the insidious "gas pods," I have no such talent to misuse. I have never toured the Lawful Police HQ building, either. Tomorrow is Sunday, and it will be the one month anniversary since my sister was arrested and executed. I am not angry; no, every day I praise the State for catching her and stopping her treason before it could be fulfilled. Imagine how horrifying it would be if the entire HQ of the Lawful Police was struck down? I shudder!

No, it is best that my sister the traitor is gone and there is no one to carry out her legacy.

Do you have any additional comments you wish to share?

I am extremely happy as a Citizen! I have instilled this loyalty and fervor for the government in my children, and I hope they will be proud of their mother and remember her as the good and upstanding patriot she is. My husband has been feeling ill more and more often these evenings, so I must make him another cocktail to help nurse him of his ailments. If we are not in the Sunday service tomorrow, it will be because I am tending to my husband. I would not know what to do without him, after all. What would any of us do without the leadership of the State and the Lawful Police?

Thank you for your participation and your display of patriotism to the Lawful State, Madison Roberts. You have scored in the top percentile! You are a Valued Citizen and the Lawful State is pleased with your service.

ACKNOWLEDGMENTS

Big thanks to John Joseph Adams for the invitation and support; thanks to Hugh Howey for hosting interviews; and my deepest gratitude and enormous thanks to Christie Yant for the fantastic editing—you truly made these stories shine.

If you enjoyed my stories, I highly recommend checking out the anthologies they were originally published in.

Ignorance is Strength: The Dystopia Triptych #1 ed. John Joseph Adams, Christie Yant, and Hugh Howey (2020)

Burn the Ashes: The Dystopia Triptych #2 ed. John Joseph Adams, Christie Yant, and Hugh Howey (2020)

Or Else the Light: The Dystopia Triptych #3 ed. John Joseph Adams, Christie Yant, and Hugh Howey (2020)

ABOUT THE AUTHOR

Merc Fenn Wolfmoor is a queer non-binary author from Minnesota, where they live with their two cats. Merc is the author of several short story collections and the novella series The Scythewulf Chronicles. They have had short stories published in such fine venues as *Lightspeed, Fireside, Nightmare, Apex, Beneath Ceaseless Skies, Escape Pod, Uncanny,* and more.

Visit their website: mercfennwolfmoor.com or follow them on Twitter @Merc_Wolfmoor.

SIGN UP FOR THE NEWSLETTER!

Want to keep up-to-date with the newest releases from Merc Fenn Wolfmoor? Join their mailing list and be the first to know when a new book or collection is available. :D

Plus, get a FREE original short story when you subscribe: https://mercfennwolfmoor.com/subscribe/

You Fed Us To the Roses: Short Stories by Carlie St. George
Final girls who team up. Dead boys still breathing. Ghosts who whisper secrets. Angels beyond the grave, yet not of heaven. Wolves who wear human skins. Ten disturbing, visceral, stories no horror fan will want to miss.

The Midnight Games: Six Stories About Games You Play Once ed. by Rhiannon Rasmussen
An anthology featuring six frightening tales illustrated by Andrey Garin await you inside, with step by step instructions for those brave—or desperate—enough to play.

Sanctuary by Andi C. Buchanan
Morgan's home is a sanctuary for ghosts. When it is threatened they must fight for the queer, neurodivergent found-family they love and the home they've created.

They Dreamed of Dead Ships by Byron M. Kain
A terrifying plague sweeps the world, and there is nowhere safe…for it comes to you in a dream about a ship. And then it is too late.

A Starbound Solstice by Juliet Kemp
Celebrations, aliens, mistletoe, and a dangerous incident in the depths of mid-space. A sweet festive season space story with a touch of (queer) romance.

Flotsam by R J Theodore
A scrappy group of outsiders take a job to salvage some old ring from Peridot's gravity-caught garbage layer, and land squarely in the middle of a plot to take over (and possibly destroy) what's left of the already tormented planet.

Find these great titles and more at your favorite ebook retailer!